“The Snitch

TO: NICK
PLEASE DO RESSUSITATE!

11-26-03

“The Snitch”

Jeffrey P. Speicher

Rockhouse Press

ISBN: 1-59268-045-3

Rockhouse Press
New York, New York

GMAPublishing.com
Check out our website
GMA is a global publishing company
Our books are available and distributed around the world and can be found on the internet at Amazon, Barnes and Noble and any major bookseller.

GMAPublishing@aol.com

Cover By: Cecilia Brendel
Manuscript Assistant: John Beanblossom

Printed in the United States of America

For Cara

Acknowledgements

To my wonderful wife, Cara, without whose support and endless encouragement, this work would never been completed. Thank you for listening to me drivel and for putting up with my annoying myopia during the completion of this book.

To, for my money, as good an editor and proofreader as those who make a living at it, my mother. May I eventually trim the fat off of my body the same way you did on this work. Also, thank you for the incredible mock-up for the cover-design which ended up being the idea for the final cover. Thank you for your time and support.

To Moses "Noodles" McDaniel, whose knowledge and experience was some of the most important material in this work. I couldn't have asked for a better guide to the lives of those less fortunate.

To J.D. Suraswadi, whose knowledge regarding weaponry and ammunition lent authenticity to many parts of this manuscript.

To my son, Tate, who is a constant source of inspiration.

To everyone at the Dallas Police Department and Internal Affairs who answered my bizarre and sensationalized questions.

To Carl Smart, whose insight and input was a tremendous help in making this manuscript whole. Thank you for your time and interest. It was most valuable.

Thanks to Glenn Mollette and GMA Publishing for offering an avenue for a young author to begin fulfilling a lifelong dream.

To Cia Brendel, the very talented artist who worked on the cover of the book to reflect the idea that I had in my head.

Chapter One

"Look, dad! I hit all seven cans in a row," Travis exclaimed, proudly.

"I think you're a natural, tiger, we'll keep practicing with the pellets and maybe you'll be ready for that .22 rifle we saw at the gun store last week," dad encouraged his six year old son.

"Alright!" the boy was positively giddy.-

Life knocks you around a little, and before you know it, you're content just being your brother's keeper.

THE SETTING SUN REFLECTED SHARPLY off of the tall, prominent glass skyscrapers that made up the downtown Dallas skyline. Between and on either side of the cluster of book-ended structures, a tangerine sunset blanketed the gaping horizon of the North Central Texas prairie. The urban heart of the city sat like an oasis surrounded by considerably smaller, insignificant brick and concrete creations. Expressways wound and wrapped themselves at the foot of the commercial Beast. Its innards were diced up by strips of tar and pavement. The streets sliced her into grid-like rectangles of varying proportions. On the outskirts, the cycle of life was continuing for two young men.

"Do you ever think about mom, Trav?"

"Of course I do, Mikey, all the time. Don't you?"

"Yeah. Sometimes I think about where we would be, ya know? Maybe we'd be like everybody else, with a house and at school and all that stuff."

"Well, Mikey, mom made some bad choices. And one of those choices was to put her need for drugs and alcohol ahead of being there for us."

"Why did she have to die, Trav?"

"Sometimes when you start down a certain path, you can lose control and things like what happened to her, happen more easily. Do ya' understand what I'm trying to say?"

"I guess so."

Travis knew that the subject would be broached again. Along with the plight of their biological father, it was a topic that came up every few weeks between the two homeless young men, these two halves of a whole, these two brothers. Travis was the younger of the two at twenty-four. The role of father-figure came naturally to him. Their father, who was the one positive influence in their lives, quickly succumbed to pancreatic cancer when they were sixteen and nineteen, respectively. Travis had been more of a father to Mike than anyone else ever since. He was a smart, cerebral kid who had excelled in school and was the likeable kind. After almost five years on the street he had hardened considerably, however, and his once bright outlook had dimmed. He perpetually fought from becoming jaded because it really had never been in his nature, and because he knew Mike didn't need that from him. Travis had lost touch with his brother several years earlier for reasons that were beyond his control. When he first landed on the street, he had no idea whether Mike was alive or dead. His fragile mind was not equipped for the brutish conditions of transience and Travis had made it his sole mission to find what he hoped was his living sibling.

It took three weeks of searching and seemingly endless inquiries and dead ends before Travis finally came upon another homeless young man who gave him his first helpful tip.

"I'm looking for this kid. Have you seen him?"

Travis revealed a four-year-old wallet-sized photo of Mike, which the young man took in his quivering, boney hand. Travis found the mousey young man's body odor almost unbearable, even though he, himself, hadn't showered in over a week.

"The picture's a little old, but he hasn't changed that much," Travis added.

The strung-out, emaciated mouse looked a little longer.

"Yeah, I think I may have seen this guy," he said.

Travis tried unsuccessfully to curb his enthusiasm, and blurted out.

"Where? When?"

"Who wants to know and what's it worth to you?"

The mouse had the gall to try to extort something from Travis.

"Listen, he's my brother and I haven't seen him in four years. He's mentally challenged and if you have any idea where he is, I'll see what I can do for you if you can tell me what you know and help me find him. I'm really not in the mood to negotiate."

The mouse mulled over Travis' statement as well as his rather nebulous and hollow proposal. There was a look of desperation and pain in Travis' eyes that the young man recognized, and he quickly found himself feeling sympathetic.

"Alright, listen, I saw him a few weeks ago down around the strip. I assume you know where the strip is?"

"Yeah, I do." Travis replied, dejected.

The strip was a location on the northwest side of the Beast where people partook in the buying and selling of flesh for fun.

The mouse continued.

"I was down there looking for a hook-up and I saw your brother with the Magic Man."

"Who's the Magic Man?" He had to ask the question, but Travis really didn't want to know what the mouse was about to tell him.

"Who do you think he is? He's only the biggest damn pimp in the city. I just assumed he was working for him."

Travis' blood began to boil. Next to being dead, this was the worst thing that Mike could've fallen into. He shook his head in a combination of ire and disbelief.

"Just go to the strip and you can't miss him. He'll stick out like a sore thumb. You'll see what I mean. I'd be careful though. He'll do just about anything to protect his 'investments'."

Travis immediately headed north for the strip. He had no idea what he was going to do when he found the Magic Man. He carried a .22 pistol in his pants pocket for protection. The problem was he had no ammunition for it. To use it would be more of a bluff than anything else. He hoped he would run into Mike first and reclaim him before it came to that. It was an unlikely scenario.

It took about fifteen minutes to reach the strip. He walked along the run down avenue looking for a "sore thumb". It was an urban ghost town. Most of the legitimate businesses had shut down or moved away from the carnal carnival. Only shells of respectable capitalist ventures remained. It was late afternoon and the whores had already come out to play. The crack-heads were circling like vultures over a dying animal looking for their next fix. The tension was palpable for more reason than one. Aside from the discomfort that came with being on the strip, he had just kicked heroin for the third time only ten days ago. The methadone was still running its course from his visit to the clinic earlier that morning. A considerable amount of his energy and self discipline was being used to suppress any and all cravings. The palms of his hands were moist. The smell of month-old garbage and cigarette butts filled the air. It was choking, the kind of environment that makes you feel dirty by simply by being in the proximity. He did take the time to appreciate the irony of a streetwalker leaning against a "No Parking At Any Time" sign. After walking about a half-mile fending off the whores, panhandlers and junkies, he made the Magic Man.

What he saw was an overdressed cartoon sucking on a thin cigar through a white filter and motioning at cars as they drove by checking out the inventory. He was African American and wore a full-length brown, tweed overcoat and a pair of shiny, white, silver-toed boots. Shielding his eyes were expensive looking gold-rimmed sunglasses, and his hair was styled into corn rows that zigged and zagged. Travis stood across the street from the flesh-peddler, watching his every move. He weighed his options which, in his mind, were twofold. He could wait, incognita, hoping that Mike would eventually present himself. Or he could approach the Magic Man directly and take his chances with the street-savvy whoremonger. A few minutes passed and Travis started to feel the anger eating at his gut and the adrenaline pounding at his chest. It was time to take action. He began walking across the strip. As he came into view of the pimp, he saw him flash the widest smile he had ever seen. It was a Fort Knox kind of smile with every brick glistening in the six o'clock sun. A few feet behind him sat a flimsy green lawn chair with an oversized rainbow colored umbrella duct taped to its back rest.

"Well, well. What can the Magic Man do for you this fine day, young man? Are you interested in making this day even better?"

He referred to himself in the third person.

Travis just looked at him, silent.

"Now, don't ansa right away, but Magic Man can tell you int'rested. Let's jus get some of the fo-mally-tees out 'da way so

maybe we can help e-chudda out? The first ting is, are you 5.0? If you are, then the Magic Man just move on down 'da street and mine my own. If you is and you don't come straight up, then you guilty of entrapment. Do we un-da-stan e-chudda?"

"I'm not a cop."

Travis detested him even more now that he had heard his opening sales pitch and disclaimer.

"Okay, okay, good 'den. Let's talk bid'ness. What kinda' ho' you lookin' fo? Magic Man got blondes, Magic Man got brunettes, and Magic Man got redheads. Now if you ain't inda' all dat, Magic Man can set you up wid wut-eva you into. Do ya' get my meanin'? Tricks is fo kids. Can ya' dig what da Magic Man is sayin?" he swiped his right index finger under his nose, sniffed and chuckled.

It was all Travis could do not do attack him right then and there. He pulled the photo from his back pocket.

"Have you seen this boy?"

Travis' abrupt inquiry that didn't concern business doused the Magic Man's happy-go-lucky tone.

"Who wanna' know?" He answered with another question.

"He's been missing for a long time and his family wants him back."

Travis' voice was gradually growing in intensity and he was taking on a scowl.

"What makes you think the Magic Man know 'dis kid, yo? Magic Man neva' even seen him bee-fo."

The denial infuriated Travis. He immediately began thinking about the useless pistol he had tucked in his pants.

"You haven't seen him, huh?"

The Magic Man removed his sunglasses revealing his eyes, one green, the other covered with a cloudy, white film.

"Dat's what Magic Man said. If you lookin' fo the 4-1-1 on this kid, you come to da wrong place. Now da' Magic Man see-rus-ly suh-jess you get on up out his grill and leave dis corner be-fo you get hurt, you dig?"

The pimp was a good salesman, but a terrible liar.

"What, you don't want to set me up with a young lady anymore, or, how about a young boy, you sick fuck!"

Travis pulled the .22 from his pocket and pressed it against the Magic Man's jugular.

"I know that you know where he is. So save your life and me some time and just tell me where I can find him."

The Magic Man was remarkably calm considering he had a gun to his throat, like it was a routine occurrence.

"You makin' a big mistake, you piece a' shit cracka'," he said, his voice risen, but his body still relaxed.

"No, you made the mistake when you took advantage of my brother. You know damn well he can't think right, and you're

selling him to these sick bastards anyway. Now tell me where he is!" He pressed the gun into his neck even harder.

"Go 'head, mutha' fucka', pop me. You ain't got da balls," the Magic Man didn't own almost all of the business on the strip by being a pushover.

His bluff called, Travis scrapped his half-baked plan and went off-the-cuff. In one motion, he lowered the pistol and with his left hand, he punched the pimp square in the Adam's apple, just like he had been trained to do in the Corps. The scum of society fell to his back on the sidewalk. He gasped and coughed, unable to breath. Travis put his heavy black boot squarely on his throat, further restricting the oxygen to his brain. The Magic Man squirmed and writhed, suffocating under Travis' foot. Every man has his limit. He managed to wheeze and whisper the words, "alright" and, "okay". Travis pulled off of his neck, but kept the boot within an inch should the pimp try anything, like reach for the gun, that was now visible, stuffed into his belt. Travis confiscated the piece before he could reach for it.

"Alright, alright. Go to dat buildin' right there and you'll fine him in one da rooms on the third flo."

Travis briefly applied more pressure as he held the pimp's .45 in his right hand.

"If you're bullshitting me, I'll be right back here to kill you with your own gun, you piece a' shit."

With that he began to backpedal, pointing the .45 at the Magic Man, who had managed to sit up, all the way across the street and into a condemned, crumbling crack-house. He flew up the stairs to the third floor and began opening doors at random.

"Mikey! Mikey! Are you in here? It's me, Travis. Where are you Mike? There was no response. He kept opening doors, checking room after room. The lewd and perverted activities he witnessed were hard, even for him, to stomach. Emaciated addicts being slapped around by sexually repressed, middle class johns was the common thread.

"Get the fuck outta' here!" chorused throughout the hallways.

He came to the third to the last door in the hallway. It was locked.

"Mike, Mikey! Are you in there?"

"Travis?" He heard his brother's voice through the door.

He took a step back and kicked the door open. There was a slovenly, obese man with disheveled white hair standing over Mike with his pants at his ankles. Travis pointed his new .45 at the john. Just because he told himself he wouldn't fire a gun again, didn't mean he couldn't use one to make a point.

"Mikey, get up. Come over here and stand behind me,"

Mikey got up and did as Travis told him. He gave Travis a big hug picking him up off of the floor. The john stood silent, frozen at the turn of events.

"Travis, I can't believe it's you. Where have you been?"

Travis accepted the hug briefly while trying to keep an eye on the sloth.

"You just stand right there, asshole." Travis moved back out of the room gripping Mike's right arm tightly pulling him along.

"What are you doin' here Trav?"

"I'm here for you Mikey. You're comin' with me. Let's go."

Travis closed the door behind them, and the two managed to make their way back down to the street. Travis raised the weapon again and pointed it at the Magic Man. He quickly realized that the leverage of the pistol was unnecessary as he saw the pimp leaning against a brick wall, rubbing his neck, helpless. All the whore pusher could do was pull his finger across his bruised and battered throat in a slow slashing motion in a pathetic attempt to give Travis notice that revenge was now his top priority. Two days later, Travis' fear of retribution from the Magic Man was quelled when he learned that the pimp had tried to recruit one too many mentally unstable whores and had been the recipient of a slug in the chest.-

Months passed and he was grateful to have found Mike, but quickly discovered what an awesome responsibility it was being his keeper. Mike was the opposite of his brother in almost every way possible. It would be fair to say that if Travis was as sharp as a tack, then Mike was as dull as a butter knife. The older brother's frame extended well over six feet and his bones were thick and sturdy. He was naturally athletic but could never fully grasp the rules of physical contests. His body had matured into one of a healthy, albeit malnourished, young man, but his mind had skidded to a halt some twenty years before. There was a great deal of irony when Travis thought of Mike and his limited intelligence. Irony, or perhaps, envy, at the fact that Mike was often too concerned with trivial minutia and child-like endeavors to fully appreciate their dire circumstance.

Nevertheless, Travis would do anything to protect Mike and harbor him from the implicit malfeasance that came with life on the streets. If nothing else, it was the reason he got up in the morning.

Chapter Two

He tore at the wrapping paper with great gusto as Travis, Dad, Mikey and mom celebrated his seventh birthday. He knew what was inside and could barely contain himself as he pulled the .22 rifle from the wrinkled heap.

"Wow, this is awesome. Thanks, Dad," he chirped with childlike exuberance.

"You're welcome son," Dad smiled.

"Aren't you going to thank your mother? It's from her too," he added.

"Oh, yeah, thanks, mom."

"Now before we use that I need to have a serious talk with you, man to man, about using guns and make sure you understand

just how important it is to know the responsibilities and dangers that come from having that gun in your hands.

"Okay, sure, dad," he humored him, too enamored with his new rifle to care.-

It's supposed to be where the heart is.

HOME WAS THE UNDERPASS OF A bridge that was just a block south out of the Beast on Lamar and Cadiz just off of I-30, the Interstate that ran from the southwest portion of Texas through the Dallas-Fort Worth Metroplex and continued northeast into southwest Arkansas. The monstrosity that was the Dallas Convention Center sat only about a football field away and served as sort of a buffer between them and the Beast's outer layer. It was just off of the R.L. Thorton exchange and was relatively isolated and quiet. Gang signs and ghetto-style art work created a rainbow of spray-painted colors on the huge pylon walls. It was a moderate space large enough for two, but no more. Large girders provided storage space just a few feet overhead. The only thing of note in the space was a stack of books which included the works of renowned minds like Nietzsche, Rand, Locke, and Marx to name a few. There was room for a couple of old eaten-away mattresses. They were small improvements over the ground on which they laid. Two adjoined plastic crates between the mattresses served as makeshift nightstands. The warm season made their thin, shabby blankets obsolete.

"Well, it looks like the maid didn't come again. I don't know what we pay her for, Mikey."

"Yeah, right, Trav," Mike replied, accompanied by a low-pitched, awkward chortle.

It was, more or less, the standard response that Mike gave when Travis' sarcasm was lost on his underdeveloped senses. The two kicked away the strewn candy bar, chip and microwavable bean burrito wrappers throughout. Home was a place where the two felt safe. Of course, safe meant two chain-linked fences, one of which had a section peeled away for passage in and out.

They settled in. Travis began perusing the pages of Sir Thomas More's *Utopia,* trying to escape a little farther from the real world. He was interested in the theories of the great thinkers. He was particularly fascinated with economic and political theory and had read most of the ponderings of Thomas Hobbes.

"How are we going to eat tomorrow, Trav?"

"Don't worry about it. I'll come up with something."

Travis read for an hour and Mike tossed small rocks through the chain-link fence before they settled in for a night's sleep. The slumber was sweet because it meant two things, they had a few hours to forget about their wayward existence, and they had survived another day.

"Are you in position Hawk 1? Over," a voice came over the walkie-talkie.

"That's affirmative, Motherhawk. I'm approximately three-hundred feet away from the target zone, locked and loaded, over," he spoke back into the radio.

"Roger that. Await further instruction, over."

The sniper surveyed the area through his modified, mounted telescope moving the crosshair laterally to familiarize himself with where he expected the target to appear.

"Hawk 1."

"Go ahead, Motherhawk, over."

"You're target is wearing fatigues. He is flanked on both sides by men in dark suits. Do you copy?"

"That's affirmative. What is their E.T.A.?, over"

"Approximately 2 minutes, over. I have a minimal wind reading. The wind is negligible. Copy."

"Roger that, over."

Hawk 1 put down his radio and adjusted his hands, arms, shoulders and torso around his rifle in order to become one with his weapon. He had wrapped the gun's sling around his elbow twice to steady it. He cradled the weapon, gently caressing the soft-touch trigger. Softly, he slid his hand between the scope and the barrel for further leverage. His mind became completely focused on the task at hand.

Motherhawk's intelligence was perfect. No more and no less than two minutes had passed when he spied his target entering the strike zone. Through his scope he tracked the target as he walked along the sidewalk. He was considerably shorter than the two men on either side of him. The target moved on and off of the crosshair's nexus. A bead of sweat rolled down the sniper's cheek. The group was almost halfway through the twelve-yard strike zone. The man in the fatigues took an extra stride ahead of his flankers leaving himself exposed. The sniper locked on to the target and fired a single .223 caliber round. The man's cranium transformed into a Pollock canvas on the white wall behind him. His lifeless body collapsed and bounced off the concrete.-

Travis' body convulsed. He awoke disoriented and sat up. His breathing was heavy and beads of sweat covered his face. His reaction to the visceral episode had woken Mike.

"Travis, are you okay?"

Still disturbed by the graphic nature of his flashback, Travis didn't respond. Mike pressed him.

"Are you having bad dreams again, Trav?"

"It's alright, Mikey, go back to sleep."

Travis lay back down in a semi-fetal position. His mind went hard to work, trying to come to terms with his past, again. It was a past that was filled with promise, a past that had the potential of ensuring a decent life, a distinguished life, a military life. At 19 years old he had become the best special operations sniper in the corps. He was a phenom who had shot through the Marine ranks since the day he stepped off of the bus at boot camp. He showed an unusual propensity with the sniper's rifle right away. When they couldn't move the practice targets back any further, they began to move Travis back. In every instance, he would hit the same, six square inch target. The bullets felt like an extension of his hand. At his peak, he could knock a chick pea off a breadboard from a half-a-mile away with barely a nick. He shot through the rigorous, five-part Marine sniper training and was assigned to special operations almost immediately. But he was too young. He was pushed too hard, too fast, pushed into seeing and doing things that he wasn't mentally or ethically equipped to handle. He began to do what so many do who are trying to bury bad memories, or, want, so desperately, to forget about the dreadful things they've done. He sought refuge in a needle. At first he managed to function with the dirt flowing through his veins, but it was just a matter of time. There was a missed target here, another one there, until finally, a staff sergeant caught him with a syringe hanging out of his arm.

A dishonorable discharge was the next step. It was the final chapter in a life that had great possibility, and the first into one that had nothing.

Chapter Three

Travis aimed at the target that sat some hundred or so feet away and fired. He continued to go through about a dozen rounds. Dad went to retrieve the target from the haystack it was mounted on.

"Seven clean hits to the body and five to the neck and head." Dad showed the target sheet to his wide eyed son who was grinning from one ear to the other.

"Awesome," he was quite pleased with himself.-

Sometimes the sunrise felt evil.

TRAVIS MOVED SLOWLY NOT WANTING to wake Mike. He changed out of one plain white T-shirt into another. He donned a plaid flannel over it. His build was slight, but not unusually so. His hair was sandy blonde. It hung down over his eyes in the front and was shorter in the back. His eyes were a pale green and round, like dinner plates. His features were sharp and well-defined. He had the kind of look that if a modeling agent were to spot him on the street, they might take a flyer on cleaning him up and putting him in front of a camera. His demeanor was unlike most in his predicament, walking lightly and sometimes even smiling slightly at certain sights and people as he passed by. If it wasn't for his soiled clothes and unwashed skin and hair, you would be hard pressed to ascertain his circumstance. It had been six years since he left his first life. Irreconcilable differences with his stepfather (he wanted to abuse him and Travis wasn't so much into being abused) and his new father's affinity for the harder liquors were the main reasons for the divorce. So it really wasn't a whole lot better than how he lived now other than the available food, occasional warmth and the shingles overhead. He never planned on ending up a permanent transient, none do, but after three months into his second life he returned home to find that his stepfather had finally decided to shake his few responsibilities and, after his last fifth of whiskey, relieved Travis and Mike's mother of her right to life, and then his own. And just like that, the boys were alone. Travis had just turned eighteen and decided to join the corps. He did so only with the understanding that Mike would be taken care of by the state until he could return and provide for the both of them.

It was about a three-mile walk north to Reverchon Park and his appointment that morning. Travis usually headed north on Lamar when entering the Beast. It was the easiest route and it meant he got to chat with a good friend of his just about everyday.

"Hey, Cubby. What da' ya' know?"

"I know that this is gonna' be a pretty good day, Travis, pretty good indeed."

Cubby was a sixty-four year old African-American man who had found a home close to the Dallas Area Rapid Transit rail that stopped underneath the vast underbelly of the Convention Center. He had bushy, cotton ball white eyebrows and a beard to match. His story was a unique one, albeit tragic. Franklin C. Cubbertson had taught history and political science at Southern Methodist University, in Dallas, in the late seventies and early eighties. He was a published author with tenure. There were only a handful of African-Americans with such a pedigree in the entire country at the time. Things couldn't have been much better for an academic until one night sent his life spiraling out of control. It was August 22, 1981, when his wife and two daughters, returning home from a soccer game, were broadsided by a pickup truck, killing all three. The driver of the truck was a drunk and escaped with only a few bruises. The accident consumed him and he began to withdraw from his friends, his family, his classes and his writing. His grief sent him down to a place so dark that he could no longer deal with the rigors of a professor's everyday life. His severance and savings gradually eroded. The family had tried to do what they could, but he had always refused charity. The truth was he didn't really want to be helped. He felt as if he deserved to wallow as a wretched and lost soul. He bounced around from place to place until landing here, below the convention center, at the DART stop for the past couple of years.

"A great day you say. Why's that, Cub?"

"You want to know why, do you? Well, I'll tell you why, my dear boy. Everyday is a great day when you've got Jesus in your heart, that's why."

Cubby had found religion in his older age and was the most cheerful person Travis had ever known, and a big reason why Travis had managed to ward off the cynicism that you would expect from a young man who had been through the things he had at only twenty-four years of age. He never understood how a man could be so happy, but it was refreshing and one of the few things he looked forward to. What Travis really liked to talk to Cubby about, however, was political theory.

"I'm reading More's *Utopia* right now. It's incredible the societies a man can create in his mind and make them sound as if they're completely plausible."

Cubby had a deep voice and he sounded like an engine trying to turn over when he laughed or chuckled.

"I'll tell you what, More sure was dreaming when he penned that one. Have you gotten to Rousseau or Locke yet?" he asked.

"Not yet, I read some more of Hobbes *Leviathan* last week and wanted to slit my wrists when I put it down."

"Don't let that pessimistic fool get to you, Trav. There was a time, especially after the accident, that I thought he may have been onto something, but I've come to realize that most people are inherently good at heart, not evil. Maybe Hobbes would've had a completely different outlook if he had found the Lord Jesus Christ and let him into his heart."

Travis was always a little skeptical when Cubby talked about Jesus Christ as some sort of cure-all, magic pill. He wasn't an atheist or anything like that. He was just one of those people who needed a little more proof. He believed that if God was so good, why would he let so much bad happen to him and Mike.

"Well, Cub, I'm on my way to meet with one of those people that is definitely not a part of that altruistic majority." Travis was enjoying talking with Cubby, as usual.

"You're meeting with that detective again aren't you?" Cubby asked, concerned.

"Yeah."

"From what you've told me about him, I would definitely try to avoid that man as much as possible, Travis."

"What can I do, Cub? Mike and I need the money to eat."

Cubby offered up a look of disapproval.

"You've offered me some of that money before, remember?"

Travis could tell he was about to admonish him, as he did from time to time.

"But I wouldn't take it. That money is dirty and any man who spends it becomes dirty. I'd rather nickel and dime my way right here from the nice people getting on and off the rail than accept his money."

Cubby could get a little righteous every now and then as well.

"Are you callin' me dirty now, Cub?"

"No, son. I'm just trying to make you think twice before you go and associate with the likes of that cop. That's all."

"If it was just for me, I might consider it. But you've gotta' remember, I'm providing for two. And Mike doesn't really care where it comes from. He just knows that he's hungry. And it seems like he's always hungry. So I can't afford to do what you do, Cub, even if I wanted to. You don't want me to start with the pick-pocketing again, do you? "

Travis had been a successful pick-pocket as a vagabond plebe, but his conscience and some preaching from Cubby put an end to that, for the most part. He still robbed when he and Mike were desperate.

"You know how I feel about that, kid. Hey, I know everybody's got to do whatever they can out here, Trav. All I'm saying is watch your back. The police in this city, especially the one you're dealing with, don't pretend to care about people like us. We can be easy targets."

Travis nodded in agreement.

"I'll be careful. I'm always careful. Do you want me to grab you anything while I'm gone?"

Cubby never refused an errand boy. He gave Travis a one dollar bill and a handful of change.

"Get me one of those chicken sandwiches…with fries," he obliged, smiling.

"You got it. But I may not be back for a few hours."

"That's alright. They don't start serving lunch for another couple of hours anyway." Cubby informed.

Travis shoved Cubby's money into his jeans pocket.

"Hey, where's Monte anyway?" Travis asked.

Monte was a schizophrenic that had attached himself to Cubby for the past six months. He was in his late twenties and had been diagnosed almost ten years ago. The unique thing about Monte was that he could remember just about anything he heard, especially lists. It was a strange, savant-like, side effect of his condition. No sooner than he had asked, they could hear the prattling of the young man rising in the distance, nearing.

"Genesis, Exodus, Leviticus, Numbers, Deuteronomy, Joshua..."

He spoke with such rapidity it was difficult to make out what he was saying.

Cubby laughed.

"Looks like we're doing the books of the Old Testament today, huh, Monte?"

Travis was both curious and amazed by Monte's unusual ability. Whenever he saw him, Travis couldn't help but attempt to pry into the labyrinth that was the savant's warped and discordant stream of consciousness.

"Hey, Monte, how are you today?"

Monte carried himself like most mentally-ill, savants do. He was hunched over with his head down and he shuffled his feet as opposed to the more efficient stride. He wore the same ragged, pin-striped sport coat that he had probably not taken off in months. The defective looked up at Travis briefly, and stopped shuffling on a dime. He changed direction and shuffled directly up to him. At no point had he lifted his head. Travis felt a little uncomfortable, and stood, looking down at the top of Monte's head, not knowing exactly what to expect. Monte was silent for almost ten seconds. He then executed an abrupt about-face and continued prattling.

"Genesis, Exodus, Leviticus, Numbers, Deuteronomy…"

"I think he likes you, Trav. I haven't seen him give anyone a once-over quite like that."

"Well, that's quite an honor, Cub. How do you know it doesn't mean the opposite? Maybe he doesn't care for me at all," Travis was a bit flip.

"You know how I know these things?" Monte rarely interjected, or spoke for that matter, so it took them both by surprise. His speech pattern was staccato and monotone.

"No, Monte, how?" Cubby asked.

"Because, I know them," he answered.

Travis and Cubby exchanged quizzical glances and continued.

"I've gotta' run now. Take it easy, Cub. See ya', Monte."

"You be good, Travis. And watch your back."

"I will, Cub."

"Don't forget my chicken sandwich and fries."

"Gotcha."

Chapter Four

Travis woke up ten minutes before his alarm clock was set to go off at 4:00 a.m. He began gathering his gear, eager to get going on his first hunting trip with Dad. Mike was asleep in the other twin bed, so he practiced the stealth that he would need when he was out in the woods tracking deer. The twelve year old amateur marksman stuffed his backpack with extra .12 gage ammunition, a camouflage vest and a thin, hunter green windbreaker amongst other things.

They were the paper that society washed there filthy hands with and tossed aside.

"SO, HOW IS THE 'ROAD' scholar this morning?"

The voice rang out from Travis' left side where he turned to see the other half of the meeting lurking behind some arboreal overhang. A figure slowly and fully emerged.

"That's very funny, Figg."

Figg, a DPD narcotics detective with the 44th precinct, was a large man standing more than six feet. He was broad through the shoulders and even the leather jacket that he wore could not hide his thick, muscular arms. His body was svelte and fit. His jet, black hair was combed back revealing a widow's peak that was exaggerated by a receding hairline. Resting on his long and pointed nose was a pair of thick, black, horned-rimmed glasses that were strangely outdated. Even odder was the fact that there were no lenses in the frames. Travis never asked him why he wore frames without lenses because he really didn't want to know the answer. It was just one of a score of idiosyncrasies about the cop he thought was better left alone. Behind the glassless spectacles, were eyes that were like two, ominous storm clouds that carried with them much tumult and danger. Beneath all of these features was a deep, chasm of a dimple sitting squarely on a cube-shaped chin that completed a sharp jaw-line. He was chomping on a toothpick as he habitually did. His teeth were stained from smoking and brown at the gums. One of his front top two teeth had been squeezed out of alignment, and jutted out from the rest.

"Are all cops as funny as you, Figg, or do you moonlight as a stand-up?"

He and Travis had been meeting a couple of times a month for almost a year. Whenever Travis needed a little cash, he made himself available for some footwork. It was usually nickel and dime stuff, a dealer here and there. Initially, this meeting didn't seem as if it was to be any different.

"You know, it still amazes me that such a smart-ass like yourself hasn't found a way off of the streets, Trav," Figg was a condescending bastard.

"I bet you lose sleep at night worrying about my situation, don't you? By the way, did you know that in several cities across the country people have been refused work as police officers because their I.Q.'s were too *high*? That's right, and the 'powers that be' were concerned that people with intelligence above that of a monkey would get bored with all that paper-pushing?" Travis quipped back.

"A man in Vermont sued," he added.

Travis had established a rapport with Figg that was unique to say the least. You almost never knew when Travis was going to step over the line and cause Figg to blow. The cop's temperament was manic, his fuse short, and Travis knew it. Yet, he continually walked the tightrope.

"You know," Figg replied, "if you didn't bump my arrest record up a good six or seven percent this year I might just have to shake you down like the common little vagrant, thief that you are. Oh yeah, I almost forgot, how's that mental defective you call a brother doin' today?"

Travis looked directly at Figg for the first time with an icy glare and an indecisive physical tenseness. Had it been anyone else, Travis would have defended Mike. This was the button that Figg knew he could press to knock Travis down a notch, and it worked without fail. The two had a perfectly antagonistic relationship, yet, they recognized each other's mutual value. But it was clear that Figg, ultimately, held the upper-hand.

Figg took notice of Travis' reaction.

"What, you wanna' hit me? Go ahead, kid, I deserve it, c'mon," Figg dropped his arms as if conceding the shot.

"Can we just get on with this?" Travis had become impatient.

"I knew you wouldn't do it. Do you know why I knew you wouldn't do it, Travis? Because your balls are made out of paper mache, that's why."

"Whatever, Figg. Do you have anything for me or what? I have things I've gotta' to do."

"Sure, sure, I know you're pressed for time," Figg replied, smug.

"I need you to finger a dealer over on the East side for me. He's been aggressively penetrating the area for several months now and has kept a good cover. None of our guys has been able to get close to him. I want you to get some information I can use on this guy and I want it fast."

"How fast?" Travis inquired.

"We want to have enough on this guy to move within a week."

"One week!?" The snitch was incredulous.

"I'm gonna' need longer than that if this guy is as protected as you say he is. What is he into, blow, "H", crank? You gotta' gimme something."

"I wish I could. That's part of the problem. We can't seem to figure out whether it's one of those things or all three. That's why I need you to see if you can try to get close to him, infiltrate his circle."

"How the hell do you expect me to do all that in one week? I mean if you guys couldn't even sniff him in months, what makes you think I'll do any better in seven damn days?"

"Well, Travis, fortunately, that's not my problem. One week and I'll throw in an extra 'get out of jail free' card. That's what I'm prepared to offer."

Travis looked up with a thick and noticeably unappreciative smirk.

"Here's a little bit of walkin' around money which I highly suggest you spend toward gathering information on the mark. I want you to call me at this number every day with progress reports." He handed Travis a business card with a hand-written phone number scribbled on it.

"Just in case you forgot," Figg referred to the cell number.

"And remember, the walls have eyes, Travis. So don't try and jerk me around on this, understand?"

Figg then handed Travis a thin file with information and photographs of the mark.

"Keep in mind that what's good for me is good for you. What's bad for me could be very painful for you."

On that threatening note, Figg retreated back into the cover of the brush. Travis stuffed the file in the small backpack that he had brought with him and left the park.

Chapter Five

THE SECOND AISLE, end, at the downtown bus station on the corner of Commerce and Lamar was always a good place to examine the materials of the mark Travis had been given. Plus, it was closer to home. The cash for the buys was typically around a $100 with a little something extra for his time. The photos revealed a mark of average height and build. He was a white male in a regular grey suit, in his mid to late thirties. His hair was a light brown and very neatly quaffed. There was only one feature that stood out on his relatively plain countenance, a mole on the left side of the nose. It was about an inch below the eye and the size of a tick. According to Figg' intelligence, the man was using the name "Vargas".

A voice rang out from a short distance and behind Travis.

"I knew I'd find you here!" Mike exclaimed, triumphantly.

He came up behind Travis and gave him a big bear hug, lifting him a foot or two off the ground. Mike greeted Travis this way on a regular basis, showing emotion like a six-or seven-year-old would. The physical display of love was the only way he knew. Travis would sometimes pretend as if he was being put out, but he couldn't help but smile just a little when he was in his brother's arms. As for knowing Mike would find Travis at the bus station, the two always rendezvoused there whenever they were apart for more than an understood period of time. Upon regaining his feet on the floor, Travis scrambled to gather his materials and scoop them into the file before Mike could see them. Travis always made it a point never to involve Mike in his activities with Figg, and Mike never had the mind to ask. He wouldn't have understood anyway, but the separation had become habit.

"Hey, Mike. What's up?"

"Nothin'. Where have you been all day?"

"I'll bet you're pretty hungry aren't you?" Travis would often change subjects on Mike to keep the conversation moving.

"Yeah," Mike rubbed his hands together in anticipation of some good eats.

"Well, I've been doing some shopping." Travis handed Mike a sandwich and a bag of chips from the nearby vending machine.

"Another chicken salad sandwich?" Mike whined.

"Its food, isn't it?"

"Barely," he contended.

"Why do you have to buy my food anyway, Trav? Are you my mother now?"

"Because if I let you do it you'd just go buy four or five candy bars and call *that* dinner," Travis muttered under his breath as he bent over to secure his bag.

"What did you say, Trav?"

"Nothin', just shut up and eat," Trav ordered, and the two sat back to back and ate like they hadn't tasted food in almost twenty-four hours.

As he stuffed his face with sandwich, Travis thought about the hand that Figg had forced on him. It was clearly the biggest assignment that he had ever been given and he couldn't help but have reservations. This was, without a doubt, the most well-dressed individual he had ever been asked to pursue. He didn't look like a dealer. He looked like an accountant. Something was very odd about this one. The problem, however, was the same as always - he felt as though he had no choice. If he refused to help Figg, he would no doubt be under the watchful eye of almost every one of the cities finest and they wouldn't hesitate to bust him for walking on the wrong side of the street. If he did as requested, there was a very real chance that this would be his last favor for

Figg and Mike would be left to fend for himself. Travis caught a glimpse of the clock on the wall.

"Let's get goin' Mikey."

"I'm not finished," Mike proclaimed.

"Then I'll see you back at home."

An antsy Travis walked toward the twin doors at the concourse exit. Mike stuffed the last quarter of his sandwich into his mouth, grabbed his backpack, and scurried to catch up with his brother.

As the two made their way back home, Travis couldn't stop thinking about the peculiarity of the man in picture. He was peculiar in the fact that he was too normal. It was, at the very least, improbable that a man carrying himself in such a tidy, middle-class fashion would be involved in heavy trafficking. As he analyzed the possibilities over and over again in his head, Travis kept reaching the same conclusion. This one was too dangerous. It wasn't worth the risk. After weighing all the pros and cons, he made a decision. He would inform Figg the next day.

"Wait a minute," Travis said. "I almost forgot. I need to get Cubby some food at Mickey's."

Mike was most unhappy with the turn of events.

"How come he gets fast food and we have to eat that stuff from the vending machine?"

"I was busy, Mikey. Just follow me and quit complaining."

"Stop being so bossy, Trav. You're not the boss a' me!"

Chapter Six

The two of them sat in the jeep just outside the house. Dad took a sip from the steamy cup of coffee. It was 4:45 a.m. and still pitch-black outside.

"C'mon Dad, let's get goin', we don't wanna' miss anything," Travis was incorrigible.

"Don't worry, son, the deer will still be there. Do you remember what I said to you when I gave you your first rifle?" he asked.

"Yeah," he answered.

"I want to have that talk with you now,"

"Okay," Travis begrudgingly agreed.

"This is one of the most important things I will ever tell you, Trav, so I want you to listen, and pay close attention, okay," Dad's face became stoic and very serious.

Travis began to understand the gravity of what his father was about to say.-

"The Turtle and the Hare" is a load of shit, even for a fable.

"MIKEY, I'M GONNA' GO USE the phone. I want you to stay here at home until I get back. Do you understand?"

"Yeah, you want me to stay here," he repeated.

"I'll be right back, okay."

"Yep."

Mikey didn't look at Travis when he responded. That concerned him because it usually meant that Mike was humoring him. Travis walked to the nearest pay phone, which was about a half-mile south from the Beast on South Lamar and used his flannel top to wipe down the pay handset before dialing. He waited nervously as the line rang three times before Figg picked up.

"Yeah, Figg here."

Travis stood up to the abusive cop.

"You don't expect me to just go along with this because you've got a couple of things on me do you?"

"Travis, are you still having doubts?" Figg responded as if he expected the call.

"Somethin' smells about this and you know it. I realize I'm not in the best position to do this, but I'm gonna' have to draw the line on this one. I won't do it."

"You're right about one thing, kid. You're not in a position to refuse anything. So let's be clear about this. Not only do I expect you to carry out your assignment, I'm prepared to take measures to make sure that you do." Figg made threats in order to ensure Travis' allegiance with regularity, but this time Travis got a sense that this threat was anything but idle. Still, he couldn't throw in his cards so easily knowing what was at stake.

"At this point, I'm content to take my chances with you instead of this 'Vargas' character. Travis' stomach twisted like saltwater taffy as he spoke.

"I'm sorry to hear you say that, kid. I guess I'm gonna have to be a little more persuasive. You don't think I'm just gonna go away do ya'? I mean, really, do you plan on watching out for Mike twenty-four hours a day?"

"What the hell! You better not lay a finger on him, Figg! He doesn't have anything to do with this. Are you a cop or not, man?"

"This is me being more persuasive, Travis. I hope I'm not making you uncomfortable. Now are you sure you won't reconsider?"

"You've lost it, Figg. You've finally gone completely off the deep end, haven't you?"

"You wanna judge *me,* kid?" Travis had lit Figg' short fuse. The crooked cop reacted as if he wanted to reach through the phone and grab Travis by the throat.

"Take a look at yourself. You're nothin' but a street urchin, a fucking waste of chromosomes. Nobody cares if you live or die, and you have the balls to judge *me*. You better take this mark or I can't guarantee what'll happen to you or your moron brother. Are we straight, boy?"

Figg's outburst was as unprecedented as it was unambiguous. Travis had never heard this level of anger and outright venom in his voice before. He was definitely shaken, but was not about to lie down. In fact, he immediately found himself pissed off and defiant as a result.

"I guess I'll just have to make myself a little less visible, huh? You forget that I know every shadow, every crevice and every corner in this city, Figg. And Dallas is a pretty big city."

"You're smarter than that Trav. If you think you-"

There was a click and then a dial tone. Figg pulled the cell phone from his ear and calmly flipped the keypad cover. He was oddly composed considering his outburst that had resulted in the impudent treatment he had just received from his snitch. Moreover, he seemed almost pleased with the exchange as he placed the phone in his coat pocket. He reclined into the plush, leather bucket seat of his car, put it into gear, and merged into a sea of traffic.

On the other end of the line, Travis had stunned himself. He was stunned at how he had just told Figg to take a flying leap. Stunned at the fact that he just told the one man in the world who could make his life even more miserable, considerably more miserable, to go fuck himself. Such brashness and irreverence was not his style, yet, not entirely a revelation. He had been shoved so neatly into a corner and felt threatened to the core. His thoughts turned immediately to the whereabouts of Mike. Travis ran back home with a sense of urgency.

"Mike!,... hey Mikey!" Travis shouted as he came upon the underpass. There was no response. From the time he left Mike to the time he got back, approximately thirty minutes had passed. Just as he had feared, the instructions he had given Mike had gone directly through his head, non-stop. Doubled-over and short of breath, Travis was just short of frantic, because he knew that if Figg found Mike, he would have the ultimate bargaining chip, plus all the leverage he would need. In his mind, he began to scour all the locations where Mike might be and charted a path to find him. The first, and most obvious place to start, was the bus station.

Chapter Seven

"There is an unwritten code of honor that is understood by every man that holds the butt of any gun to his shoulder. There are only three elements to this code of honor," Dad held three fingers up firmly.

"The first is for self defense. If you feel your life or the lives of your loved ones are in danger from another person or an animal, it is okay to use your weapon. Second, if you shoot an animal, like we're about to go and do, you take what ever you shoot home and you feed yourself, and/or your family with the meat of that animal. You never hunt purely for sport or to kill for the sake of killing. The final, and most important part of the code, is that you never, and I mean ***never,*** *point your weapon at another human being out of anger, or for fun, or for any other reason if*

that person is unarmed or not a threat to you. Do you understand the things I have just told you?"

Dad's demeanor and body language took on a stringency that the boy had never seen before. He was left wide-eyed and speechless save for the words, "yes, sir."

"Good, I don't want you to ever forget that," he said as he started the jeep.

"I won't," he said as earnestly as a twelve year old could.

Dad looked over and smiled at Travis, and the two headed out on their first of the precious few hunting trips they would have together.

You can run, but...

AS HE GALLOPED ALONG THE ASPHALT, Travis found himself with his head on a swivel. He still had the cash that Figg had given him and he looked for a cab, but none was in the area. Even if there were, cabbies rarely picked up people like Travis. As desperate as he was to find Mike, he had to be constantly vigilant of not only Figg, who rode in an unmarked car, but the patrol cars as well. He had no idea who, or how many other cops were in cahoots with Figg. He hadn't gotten a quarter of a mile before a cacophony of flashing red, white and blue rollers came into panorama only a few hundred yards ahead. They were coming toward him with some speed. Travis darted to his left and was immediately out of sight behind the dumpster that sat in the alley behind an old, six-story brownstone. Breathing heavily and fearing having already been spotted, he slid down into a crouched position and hoped he was just being paranoid. And with the swoosh of sirens and the churning of pistons as the cars sped by, it appeared as if he was just that. It was a small relief, but a welcome one as he peeked around the bin and continued on his way.

There were four main thoroughfares between Travis and the station. And as he approached the first, there were mixed feelings of both being safer in numbers as pedestrian traffic picked up, but also greater exposure to the trolling flat-hats. Interloping with the other-worlders was always difficult for Travis. He usually tried to keep his distance from them as if he were surrounded by a force-field of guilt and melancholy. They were not eager to close the space between them either. This was not like other days, however, and Travis found himself sidling up to the crowd quite nicely as he crossed the intersection. He was like a remora fish attached to a shark's dorsal fin as the group made their way to the curb. It was, in his opinion, the only time they were of any use to him. Once across, it was back to hugging the wall with an occasional glimpse into the glass reflections of the storefronts to evaluate his clandestine manner.

He was progressing at a decent pace and seemingly unnoticed as he approached the second crossing when he felt a hand lay on his left shoulder. His heart skipped double-dutch and he swung around.

"Travis!" the man spoke. Where have you been hiding, kid? I've missed you."

It was Espinosa. Espinosa was the South-side's resident smack dealer and the proverbial thorn in Travis' side as he was always around to check-up on Travis and see whether or not he either had or could be swayed into "falling off the wagon". The junk had always been Travis' Achilles heel. *It* was more likely to separate him from Mike than any pimp or rogue cop. It almost had a couple of times before he kicked it the last time. If Travis feared anything, it was the junk.

This smallish man of no more than five and a half feet was of Hispanic ancestors and in his mid-thirties. He wore a cheap blue warm-up suit lined with white stripes over a white tank top marked by a sizeable mustard stain. The jacket was unzipped to allow his ample belly to hang without discomfort. His goatee was shaved with precision and his sideburns extended down to the crest of his swarthy, rotund cheeks. An earring hung from one ear- there would probably be another in his right ear had it not been severed by an unhappy client some years ago. Gold chains spewed from around his neck while more fingers were adorned with rings than not. As a rule, this was the absolute last person Travis wanted to see. And at this particular moment, given his soaring adrenaline level combined with his need for haste without impediment, Travis felt the urge to push Espinosa into traffic and be done with it.

A cooler head prevailed and Travis thought he would simply try to proceed as if the entire encounter had never occurred.

"Whoa, whoa!" Espinosa spoke with a heavy accent.

"Where are you headed in such a hurry, Trav?"

He tried to catch up with a now swiftly walking Travis.

"I don't have time for this, Espinosa. I'm still not interested in anything you got."

"Hey, wait a minute, Travis, how many times have I got to tell you, call me Espy, hombre."

"Whatever."

"I just want to talk to you, man. You know, to see how you're doin'. I was hoping maybe we could help each other out."

Espinosa had to run to get in front of Travis and to try to slow him down. He nearly tripped as he walked backwards.

"Stay out of my way, Espinosa. I mean it, get lost. I don't have time for your bullshit!"

"Hey, c'mon, Trav, that's no way to talk to a friend, man. Would you slow down for just a second?" Espinosa's request went unheeded.

"You look like your runnin' from something or somebody. Are you? Are you in trouble, Trav?"

"God Dammit, as if you care. Get lost… Now!" Travis was reaching a boiling point.

"It's Figg, isn't it? You messed with that psycho didn't you?" Espinosa said with a wry smile.

Travis stopped on a dime and took the portly Latino by the collar and slammed him into one of the storefront entryways.

"What do you know about Figg, you son of a bitch? *WHAT DO YOU KNOW*!?" Spit flung from Travis' mouth, now nose to nose with Espinosa.

The fury and anger in Travis' voice threw Espinosa for a loop. It was such a drastic departure from the normally mild-mannered, affable personality that he had grown accustomed to.

"Calm down, man. Trav, just calm down." Espinosa pleaded for his health.

"I don't know anything, Travis. I swear, nothing, nothing. I just hear things, ya' know. I just heard that you and him had an arrangement, ya' know, that sometimes you helped each other out that's all, I swear, that's all, man. I haven't seen the guy in months."

Travis was content with Espinosa's denial. He didn't have time to argue the point anyway.

"You just stay away from me from now on. Got it? I don't want to see you anymore. I'm a different person now and there is no room in my life for you and what you're offering. So, if you see me on the streets from now on, you'd be smart to just turn around and walk in the other direction."

Travis gave Espinosa a small shove before releasing his collar.

"I can appreciate that, Trav. Really, I can. But let me just remind you that friends are hard to come by out here and some day you're gonna' need a favor and I won't be there to help you out, hombre."

"You're not my friend and you never were. Let's make that perfectly clear while we're at it. Now get the hell outta here."

Espinosa walked away without saying another word and Travis' attention returned to getting to Mikey.

Now past the second crossing, Trav continued on at a very brisk pace. He was still checking out everything going on around him and felt confident that he was progressing without being tailed. Every fifty yards or so, Travis would take mental snapshots of the cars that were cruising down the street alongside him in an attempt to make sure he wasn't being followed. He thought it would be simple to decipher between regular traffic and a police sedan. Just about a half block behind him, however, was a car crawling along in the middle of traffic like a turtle surrounded by a herd of spry gazelles. It was a maroon SUV that had been lagging behind the normal flow of traffic for several blocks. Travis noticed the truck and his suspicion had begun to grow. If it was present in the next snapshot, it would be time for him to take immediate, evasive action. In other words, run like hell. His heart began to pump. It pumped faster-faster still as he prepared to kick it into high gear. He decided he would take ten more steps and then look again. One…two… three…four… he heard the sound of an engine becoming louder and louder, it was coming closer, his blood pressure pumped wildly and his body pulsated with anticipation. …seven…eight…. He couldn't afford to wait any longer. He whipped around just in time to see the SUV ride up onto the curb bearing down on him like a heat seeking missile. Travis sprung headfirst and rolled up against a storefront brick wall. The truck came within a foot or two of his body, and was close enough to catch Travis' fingers that were extended from the dive. He shrieked as the SUV tire rolled over two digits on his left hand, flattened a stop sign and bounced messily off of the curb back onto the street and fishtailed back under control. Ignoring the pain, Travis rolled back toward the street desperately trying to make out the license plate number, but the exhaust smoke blurred his view. The truck turned quickly to its right and disappeared down a side street. He rolled over onto his back and lay there, numb. He stared skyward, his eyes glazed over. There was a strong smell of burnt rubber in the air as the attack vehicle had left two twenty foot tread marks. He could faintly hear a smattering of voices as a few concerned other-world witnesses hovered over him. He laid there, catatonic, for a minute or two before he was coaxed into sitting up. He began to gather his wits, nodding slowly if only to humor the good-Samaritans when he noticed one of them on a cell phone.

"Who are you calling? Who are you talking to?" Travis barked, still not completely lucid.

"Just relax, buddy, I've got some help on the way," he replied.

Travis tried to get up and the pain shot to his left mid-section and his left hand. He stumbled backed to the ground. The other-worlders tried to keep Travis subdued as he struggled to get up again.

"Lemme go. I don't need to go to the hospital. Get your damn hands off me!"

Travis managed to struggle to his feet. He was in a tremendous amount of pain as he cradled his bad hand in his good one and leaned in a pronounced fashion over what was likely a bruised or broken rib or two. Fortunately, his legs were still functioning at close to one hundred percent and he shuffled forward like a wounded animal looking for shelter.

Chapter Eight

"Go deep, Trav. Mikey, you cover him, okay," Dad held the football securely in his right hand and barked out, "hut, hut!"

Travis darted off the imaginary line of scrimmage and made his way by Mikey, who seemed intent on trying to pull him to the ground, and ran another twenty yards expecting the pass from Dad. He looked back to see his father laying on the ground, the ball a few feet from his hand.

"Dad, what's wrong?" he screamed sprinting back to his father's side.-

If the hatchling fails to scale the beach to the ocean waters, it will be eaten by predators.

AS DUSK APPROACHED, HE FELT more vulnerable than ever before. He sat on the second floor fire escape platform, his mind deluged by myriad of questions. What was so important about this Vargas? What was it about this particular person that had Figg so worked up? There was a small sense of consolation when he thought of how Figg' drastic reaction to his refusal seemed to justify his rejection of the assignment. His overall mood, however, was being directed by negative feelings. Tears welled in his eyes as he thought about his predicament and his brother, who he still couldn't account for. Not to mention the pain he was in. His pinky and ring fingers were throbbing now that the shock had worn off. The same could be said for his side that he had managed to wrap in a long, blotched piece of cloth picked off of a pile of nearby debris. He had decided that he would wait for nightfall before moving again, and that time was nigh. He thought about his Dad.

Travis cautiously descended down the escape ladder. As he delicately grabbed the rungs, he was fairly sure that his fingers were broken. He stepped cautiously back out into the open. Even though it would take a little longer, Travis decided that he would stick to the side streets the remainder of the way. Unable to jog, even lightly, he walked as fast as his aching side would allow. He was beginning to come to the realization that even if Mike had been at the station earlier, the likelihood of him still being there grew slimmer with every passing minute. What should have taken him twenty minutes was now creeping up on two hours, but he couldn't take any other course of action until he had ruled out the station.

He could finally see the bus station lights on the horizon. It was just a matter of seconds now before he would find out what his immediate future had in store. If Mike was there, he would simply buy two one-way bus tickets out of town and take his chances starting anew in another city. If Mike didn't turn up, then he would keep searching, even if it killed him.

He hadn't realized how muggy it was until the cool, air conditioning swept across his face as he entered the station. Their spot was at the far end of the large concourse area to his immediate right. Upon arriving, he saw what looked like a body slumped over, sleeping, in the seat that Travis always occupied. He could only make out a shoulder as the seat faced the opposite direction from where he was approaching. It was a broad, rounded shoulder consistent with Mike's. Although he was anxious and hopeful that he had corralled his big brother, he moved slowly, scanning the surroundings and all those within it. He was closing in on his target. He desperately wanted to shout out "Mikey!" but fear and paranoia gripped his tongue.

Travis crept to within yards of the slumbered shape whispering “Mike,…Mikey”. He got no response. Only a few feet away now, he recognized the back of his head. It was Mike. Gingerly, he slid into the seat and was now back to back with his brother.

“Mike, wake up, man! Wake up! We gotta’ get outta’ here. We gotta’ get outta’ here, now!”

Still, Mike didn’t respond. Travis knew he was a heavy sleeper. He raised his voice several octaves.

“Wake the fuck up, Mike! I’m serious!”

Nothing.

Travis turned his torso almost 180 degrees in his seat. It felt like someone was jabbing a dozen knives into his side. Again, he implored, “Mike!” this time with a sturdy shove to Mike’s exposed shoulder.

“Who beh ta wa?”

Startled and half asleep, Mike jerked from his awkward recline and muttered something incoherent.

“Get your stuff together, Mike. We’re leaving right now.”

“Right now? Where, back home?”

Mike rubbed his eyes and stretched his arms.

“No, I mean were getting on a bus and going as far as it’ll take us.” Travis spoke impatiently and with supreme urgency.

"Wait a minute, Trav. What is going on? I don't want to leave. What's wrong with staying here?"

"You have no idea, Mikey. I'm dead serious, come with me now and I'll explain on the way." Travis was understandably frustrated with his dim-witted sibling.

"But I'm hungry, Trav." Mike complained like the small child that was in his head.

Travis rolled his eyes at Mike's impetuousness, but didn't object as he realized that he could use some nourishment before the trip as well. He winced as stood up reaching deep into his pocket for a dollar or two.

"Get a couple of candy bars and drinks out of the machines. Hurry! Then meet me right there at that ticket window okay." Travis pointed to the window on the end. Mike looked and nodded.

Chapter Nine

"Hey, there's my marksman," Dad's voice was fragile and weak as he lay in his hospital bed with his back and head propped up, a morphine drip from his right arm.

"Hi, Dad," Travis said, meekly, with his hands stuffed firmly in his pockets. He approached the bed and sat by his father, head hung low enough to lick the ground.

"What's the matter, kiddo," Dad tried to broach the subject of mortality and death with his teenaged son.

Travis looked up as tears trickled from both eyes and he lightly draped his left arm over his Dad's stomach and dropped his head on his chest.

"Hey now, we're not gonna' have any of that in here," he said softly, his own eyes becoming a little glassy.

"You're my hunter, I need you to be strong now, Trav. You're gonna' go live with your mom now. I had a long discussion with her, and she's promised me that she is gonna' take care of you and Mike like a real mother should, but you're gonna' have to help her, Trav. She'll have a hard time with Mike. That's why you have to make me a promise, Trav. Look at me, Trav. Promise me that you'll take care of your brother. Above all else, you make sure that your brother is taken care of."

"Okay, Dad, I promise," Travis whimpered.

"He is really gonna' lean on you now. You're strong and you're smart. You always have been." Dad's voice grew weaker with every word.

"I don't know if I'm ready for this, Dad. I don't want to live with mom again. She's still hangin' around with that guy that treats me and Mikey real bad. He doesn't care about us or mom. That's why we came to live with you in the first place. I need you. What are we gonna' do without you?" he said, sniffling.

"You know what?" Dad's tone lifted a bit, "you just remember that code I told before we went on our first hunting trip. You do remember it, don't you?"

"Of course I do." Travis began to sob, not willing to embrace the fact that the end was near.

"You apply the basic ethics of that code into everything you do in life, and you'll be just fine. You understand me, Trav?" Dad

was trying to impart as much wisdom and guidance upon Travis as he could before he died.

"Yes, dad, I understand."

Travis' head still rested on his Dad's chest as his tears had formed a wet spot on the hospital garment Dad wore. And then there was silence. He hadn't noticed the heartbeat in his ear until it was gone. There was the buzz of a monitored flat-line. He looked up at his Dad's face, and he was no more.-

"ALRIGHT THEN, TWO ONE WAY tickets to Memphis comes out to $87.96," the ticket salesman warbled through the archaic microphone.

"That bus leaves in five minutes, right?" Travis reaffirmed.

"Yeah, you better get goin'. I think they're about done boarding."

Travis hastily counted out ninety dollars in cash and dropped it into the metal tray under the glass partition. Mike's eyes were as wide as silver dollars.

"Where'd you get all that money, Trav?"

"Don't worry about it. Besides, that was just about all of it anyhow. Now go,go,go!" Travis gave Mike two or three firm nudges toward the boarding area. Mike still hadn't noticed that Travis' was walking in a considerably contorted fashion as the two made their way through the swinging glass doors, across the loading zone and onto the bus that would take them to a new city and, hopefully, a better life.

Mike saw two empty seats toward the back on the left side of the aisle.

"Right over here, Trav, over here." Mike was proud to have spotted the vacancies before Travis did.

He took the window seat and pressed his face against the window, Travis eased into the seat on the aisle. He put his head back and let out a long breath. It was a release, a release of fear mostly, but also one of accomplishment. He felt like he had triumphed over not only Figg, but all the cruelty and injustice that the rogue cop embodied. There was no guarantee that things were going to be significantly better in Memphis, but Travis knew that it had to be an improvement over what they were leaving behind. The unmistakable sound of the bus door hydraulics closing put a smile on Travis' face, and as the driver began his announcements over the P.A., a peace came over his visage and he let himself relax for the first time in nearly forty-eight hours.

The respite was short-lived as the bus had just rolled out of the station when it came to a sudden, jolting stop. Travis looked up front to see what was going on. He saw the driver reach for the handle that opened the door. In what seemed like slow-motion, he saw a head emerge from the partition that separated the entry steps from the front row of seats. It was Figg. He flashed a badge in the face of the driver and said a few short words before he began to make his way down the aisle, scanning every face along the way. A murmur came over the bus as the passengers were both curious and a little intrigued by the interloping law man.

"Hey Trav, look, it's that cop we know. What's his name again?" Figg had shown up, unannounced, at home several months ago to discuss an assignment.

As usual, however, Mike was oblivious to the impending danger. Meanwhile, Travis sat in his seat, frozen, partly out of shock and partly out of pure exhaustion. Helpless to elude Figg, he could do nothing other than lay-in-wait of whatever he had in store for them.

"I'm glad to see you boys are putting my money back into the local economy." Figg cracked as he came to a stop only a few feet from Travis.

"Unfortunately, I'm afraid that you're gonna' have to postpone this little trip for at least a few days." Figg pulled his jacket back at the waist to reveal a .40 SW pistol tucked neatly into its holster.

"Why don't we get off this bus and take a ride. What da' ya' say, fellas?"

Travis, exasperated, put his head back in utter resignation.

Mike was clueless.

"We haven't done anything wrong. Tell him, Trav'. We haven't done anything. Do we have to go to jail, Trav?"

Travis held his head in his hands. He was trying to think of something off-the-cuff to keep Mike from getting scared.

"It's alright, Mike. He's an actor. He's practicing for a show that he is going to be on and we get to help him practice. Let's go with him, come on."

Figg smiled.

"You're so thoughtful, Travis, trying to protect the moron from the evil that men do."

Travis and Mike got up slowly and made their way to the front. Figg followed closely while trying to quell the apprehension of the thirty-some passengers.

"Everything's fine folks, these two are in police custody. We'll be out of here in a few seconds and you people can be on your way. Say 'Hi' to Elvis for me when you get there."

Some of the other-worlders laughed at the bad joke. Travis wanted to slap each one of them silly. He had no idea what Figg had planned for him and Mike as he led them off the bus and around the corner of the building onto a dimly-lit and very narrow side street. The man was so unpredictable. Was he just going to shoot them both in the back of the head and go on about his business? In any case, Travis realized that at this point, he had nothing to lose. He decided, for Mike's sake as much as for his own, to put on the facade of fearlessness. He was going to play the only card he had which was to try to engage Figg in a mental game of chess and pray that he bit. As they walked down the shadowy street lit only by a faint moonlight, Travis made the first move,

"You know what, Figg?"

"What's that, kid?"

"You just made a big mistake taking us off that bus."

"Oh, you think so?" Figg' reaction was one of amusement.

"Why's that?" he asked in a sarcastic tone to humor him.

Travis realized he hadn't prepared for said chess match and his mind raced to come up with a credible reason.

"Because we were willing to get out of town and not use the information we've gotten on you over the last 24 hours." He was satisfied with his ad-lib.

"Is that right? Well, maybe I shouldn't take any chances and shut you urchin-fucks up for good."

Suddenly, Travis hated his ad-lib. He tried moving another pawn.

"If you were going to do that, you would have offed us already."

This time, the manic Figg lashed out,

"You don't have a fuckin' clue what I'm prepared to do."

Initially, Figg' outburst startled Travis, but he quickly realized that he had succeeded in at least getting under the skin of the sociopath. His satisfaction, however, was quickly erased when Figg moved to grab Mike by the hair and forced him to his knees. With cat-like quickness, he pulled the gun from his holster and pressed the cold steel barrel against Mike's left cheek.

"Did you expect me to do that?!" Figg roared as he pulled Mike's head back further.

"I might just kill this retard right now!" Figg was speaking so wildly that the toothpick went flying out of his mouth and drool spilled from his lower lip like a rabid dog.

"He's not of any use to anybody. Is he? I mean, what's to keep me from splattering his brains all over the pavement?"

"Trav, what's goin' on? I don't think I wanna' help with this show." Mike held his hands out toward Travis, literally reaching for help.

Travis found himself unable to exhale. He never expected Figg to overreact to such a spectacular degree. All he could manage to softly verbalize was, "Figg, c'mon man, you don't wanna do that." He realized it was a terribly meager response, but his brain had stopped working on all but the most basic of cylinders.

"Don't tell me what I want! Don't ever tell me what I want! And don't ever perceive to know what I will and will not do! Do you understand?" Figg redefined vehemence speaking with unbridled passion and energy.

"Alright, alright, I'm sorry. Just let him up. Please!"

And just like that he raised Mike up the same way he had taken him down, put his .40 SW back in its holster and wiped the excess saliva from his mouth.

"Let's go," he said, so cheerfully it was eerie.

His upbeat tone sounded as if he was convinced that the episode that *just* occurred, hadn't.

Out of the darkness, Travis could see the back end of a mid-sized sedan parked close to the only street light that was fully lit and he realized that they were not going to die in the street. While the sight did give him a little solace, he understood that in the future he was going to have to be a little more careful before he moved his chess pieces. When they reached the car, Figg reached behind his back and pulled out two pairs of hand-cuffs from his belt.

"Mike, I want you to put these on Travis, with his hands behind him. Do you think you can handle that?" Figg was merciless when it came to exploiting Mike's low I.Q. Once the cuffs were secure on Travis' wrists, Figg immobilized Mike's hands and arms the same way.

"Hey, these things hurt. They're too tight. C'mon, take 'em off, they hurt." Mike whined upon deaf ears.

Figg continued by pulling two bandanas from his back pocket and securing them tightly around their eyes. He then proceeded to stuff them one by one into the backseat as he took the front seat. They heard the voice of a second man in the driver's seat chime in.

"Ready?"

"Yeah, let's go" Figg said. The driver put the car in gear and they pulled away from the curb.

Chapter Ten

A group of about thirty, dress-black, mood-somber, huddled under a makeshift tarp cover that kept them and Dad's casket dry from the winter rain. As the preacher eulogized, Travis gazed at the long wooden box and couldn't believe his hero lay inside. He fully expected him to push it open and pop out declaring that the doctor's were wrong. He was too strong to die. Mike nudged his left arm,

"Hey, you wanna' get some chocolate ice cream, double scoop, after this thing is over."

Travis lowered his head and began to weep. He looked up at his mother. She held a handkerchief to her eye, but it seemed to him like she was merely acting the part. Her new love interest, and his future stepfather, was disrespectfully draped all over her while sneaking swigs from a silver flask. He made a soft remark into her ear and Travis read his lips,

"Let's move this along, padre."

He smiled as he spoke. Right then, Travis realized his life would never be the same again.

The show's the thing.

TRAVIS COULD HEAR THE PITTER patter of the warm Texas rain coming down harder and harder on the windshield of the car as they sped through traffic. They were both lying on their sides in the back seat. It smelled like old, moldy tennis shoes and a rank amalgamate of everything that had been brought in from the city sidewalks and streets. His concern turned to Mike. He could only imagine what was going through the mind of a young man with the mentality of a small boy at such a moment.

"Hey, Mikey. Hang in there, big brother. You're doing fine. Everything's gonna' be fine. Do you hear me, Mike? It's all just for show, don't be afraid. You remember when we were kids and we would play cops and robbers? This is the same thing, Mikey. Okay?"

"Alright, Mikey here's your pistol. Now, I'm gonna' pretend like I just robbed the bank and this sack here is full of money, understand?"

Travis, 9, always had to explain the scenario to Mikey, 12, whenever they played 'bank robbery'.

"Yeah, I remember now, Trav," Mikey replied.

"Okay, good. When I come out of the back door, I want you to chase me down and shoot me dead. You get to be the hero of the game."

"Alright, I like being the hero!" Mikey jumped up and down and dropped his toy six-shooter.

Travis went into the house.

"Ready, Mikey? Here I come."

Travis burst through the screen door holding a white sack full of dirt and rocks and scampered off trying to flee the scene of the hold-up.

"Pow, pow, pow, pow," Mikey ran after his little brother and tried to gun him down.

I'm not gonna' let…"

Figg cut Travis off.

"No, Mike, oh no, you need to be afraid. You should be shitting your pants is what you should be doing."

"Figg, you son-of-a-bitch!"

"Shut up, Travis!" He felt the .40 tracing the outer part of his ear all the way down to the lobe.

Figg continued, "You see, Mike, your brother made a big mistake and now you're gonna' have to pay the price for his miscalculation. All I asked of him was a little favor, and not only did he refuse, but he was very, very rude to me. And that hurt my feelings." Figg spoke to Travis using Mike as a convenient conduit.

"Is this part of show, Trav? Why don't you just do the favor, Trav?"

Mike's question brought a look of frustration to Travis' half-covered face.

Figg jumped at the opportunity to keep playing his little game.

"Yeah, Trav, why don't you just do the favor?"

"It's more complicated than that, Mikey. It's more than just a favor," Travis tried to explain.

As the swish of the tires through the rain soaked streets became more pronounced, Travis began trying to make a mental map of where they were as well as where they might be going. The loud music coming from the live bands through the open doors of the bars and open-air stages made it quite clear that they were close to the Deep Ellum district on the East side of downtown. The noise level was muted enough that Travis could tell they were a block or two away from the pedestrian-heavy areas of Elm, Commerce and Main streets, the main thoroughfares through Deep Ellum. Travis felt a centrifugal force pushing his body to the left, indicating a hard right turn. As the guitar licks and drumbeats quickly faded, he knew they had passed the Generation X music and art center on the south side. Judging from the distance between where the noise was inaudible and where they had turned, he was confident that they had accessed the I-30 East merge. As the car accelerated, he got his confirmation. They continued at a high rate of speed, but Travis could only guess their miles per hour. When they eventually exited the freeway, he surmised that they had traveled roughly three or four miles southeast of downtown. As Travis continued to try to hone in on their location, Figg interrupted.

"Take a right at the next signal, right here."

Intentionally or not, Figg had managed to irreparably spin Travis' mental compass as they car pulled onto what sounded like wet gravel and came to a stop.

"You two stay down. Keep your heads down! If either one of you makes a sound, well, gosh, I think you know not to make a sound." Figg chuckled as he exited via the passenger side door.

As he slammed the door shut, Mike began to whimper like a hungry puppy seeking shelter from the rain.

"I'm scared, Trav. It's hard to breath. Why do we have to have these things on?" he sniveled, referring to the cuffs.

"And I can't see. It's so dark, Trav. You know I don't like the dark, Trav."

"Hey, c'mon, Mikey. You gotta' be brave for me now. You gotta' help us make this show really good, okay?"

Travis tried desperately to ease Mike's troubled mind. It was enough for the time being. Mike stopped grumbling. All that was left at that point was a blind silence that left Travis with a profound sense of shame, shame over the fact that it was his actions and his dealings with Figg that had them hand-cuffed and blindfolded in the backseat of a fetid city squad car. But what really put a knot in his stomach was the fact that he had failed Mike. He couldn't bear to think of the trauma that his brother was experiencing right now because of him. The overwhelming guilt caused him to try to soothe Mike even further. He spoke as softly as he could.

"I'm here Mikey, I'm not gonna' let them…"

"Shut up!" The driver took the butt-end of his gun and brought it down with force on the temporal portion of Travis' skull. The pain came in ringing waves, each more severe than the last. He was dazed and felt as if he might lose consciousness. He successfully fought to stave it off. He could feel the warm blood trickling and meandering around his right ear and onto his cheek.

As the excruciating pulses of pain began to ebb, he heard a car door open and close.

"Alright, let's go."

The tread of the tires grabbed the soggy gravel and spit it out as the car returned to smooth pavement. In the backseat, Travis, with his bruised ribs, broken fingers and brand new concussion, was feeling like he had gone ten rounds with the heavyweight champion of the world. In the midst of his pain, he thought about the last discussion he had with Cubby, and how they talked about Thomas Hobbes' *Leviathan.* Even though he had warned him to stay away from Figg, he wanted his friend and teacher to see what it really looked like with "the absence of law and order", and just how easily the life of a man could be, "solitary, poor, nasty, brutish and short."

Wherever they were going was considerably less important to him now. His level of discomfort had peeked and he had temporarily lost the desire to do anything other than cooperate. He lay in wait for the car to reach its destination. His mood had soured as he was completely helpless, hateful and guilt-ridden. He thought about his Dad.

Chapter Eleven

Travis and Mike approached the house as they ended their walk home from school. The stepfather had is head buried under the hood of the '67 model speedster that he loved more than anything. He heard the boys nearing and emerged from his sweetheart's bowels, oil smudges and all. There was a three-quarters imbibed forty-ounce bottle of malt liquor resting on the black tool box by his feet. He wiped his hands with a blackened cloth and slurred as he spoke to them.

"Get your ass inside and check on your mother, Travis. I don't want that bitch smoking all my dope again."

"Whatever." Travis replied.

"Hi, Mikey. How are you doing?" the stepfather intentionally slurred his already drunken speech badly, mimicking the voice pattern of a mentally challenged individual.

"Shut up, you worthless shithead," Travis did a one-eighty, expanded his moderate chest and took two steps toward the stepfather. He was face to face with him.

"You want to take a swing at me, punk?" the stepfather's breathe reeked of barley.

"I told you not to talk to him like that." Travis' heartbeat raced as he prepared for a fight.-

The devil appears in many forms.

"GET 'EM INSIDE AND PUT 'em in the bathroom," Figg's directive was terse.

The driver pawed Mike first. He had fallen in between the seats and it was proving to be somewhat difficult to extract him from the car.

"Hey, that hurts. Ouch! Stop it. That hurts!" Mike shouted naively, thinking the driver might actually ease up. The car door shut and Travis was alone for five or six seconds before he felt the driver's massive, vice-like talon, latch onto his arm and yank him from his face down position in the backseat.

The rain had lightened to a drizzle and they mudded just a few yards to the cover of a small tin canopy. The rain had brought with it a cooler air. Still blindfolded and cuffed, Travis and Mike were shoved through a narrow single door opening and began to walk what seemed like a long distance for being indoors. Eventually were led into another much smaller room. The sound acoustics made it clear that they had been taken into a smallish bathroom. Travis was cuffed to the piping underneath the toilet and Mike to the shower curtain rod.

"I'm sure you boys are anxious to see your accommodation and settle in a little bit," Figg, again, was generous in his use of sarcasm. He removed the blindfolds to reveal a filthy, dank and malodorous setting. It was illuminated by a single, exposed bulb that swung like a pendulum tossing chiaroscuro to and fro. The tub was rusted brown and covered with strata of filmy growth. There was, a brave water roach that hadn't scurried out of sight with the others when the light came on. The floor was covered with broken tiles; not a single tile was completely in tact. The toilet was unbearable. It lacked a cover of any kind and hadn't been touched by a cleaning product in years. Travis was thankful to get a look at Mike and see that he was physically unharmed. The same couldn't be said for Travis, and Mike took notice.

"You have blood on your face! What happened to you, Trav?"

The blood that had come from the pistol whip had forked into a trident-like pattern spanning his right cheek and chin. The dried platelets had taken on a burgundy hue.

"Don't worry about me, I'm fine," Travis lied. "How are you doing?"

"I'm okay I guess," Mike said. But I wanna' go home. I don't want to be in this T.V. show anymore. It's no fun."

"We'll get to go home soon, Mikey. I just want you to know that you shouldn't be scared. It's their part in the show to try to scare us. That's all they're trying to do, okay? Mike, whatever happens from here on, I want you to remember that this is all pretend. You think you can do that for me?"

"I guess so. But ask 'em how much longer they're gonna' need us for the practicing cause I'm getting hungry and this is no fun."

"You got it, buddy."

Travis was exhausted. It had been the longest day of his short life. He wasn't sure of the time, but estimated it at close to midnight. Mike began to doze. Somehow he had managed to find a level of comfort suitable for sleeping sitting on the tub leaning against the wall with his arm hanging from the shower rod. Travis' issue had more to do with the olfactory nightmare coming from the toilet that was only a couple of feet from his head. His extreme physical and mental fatigue superceded his sense of smell to such a degree, however, that he was soon met with a well-deserved slumber.

Chapter Twelve

THE FOLLOWING MORNING TRAVIS awoke feeling like he had been run over by a semi. The right side of his head had a knot the size of an alpine mogul and was accompanied by a mighty ache. His untreated ribs and fingers were not getting any better. He didn't have time to dwell on it, though, because he had to begin plotting for what was surely going to be another long and unpredictable day.

Mike awoke shortly after Travis and the two sat idly awaiting some sort of action from their captors. Travis looked at Mike's cuffed hand and arm that extended at a forty-five degree angle to the curtain rod. It had lost all of its color save his hand which had turned purple.

"Mike, stand up on the tub there and see if you can get your head and shoulders above your hand. Will you do that for me?"

"It feels weird, Trav. It feels like my arm isn't even there."

"I know, Mikey. That's why I want you to stand up, so your blood can flow and it won't feel as weird."

"Okay."

Mike got up and stood on the edge of the tub. When he did, Travis noticed Mike's hair being blown about. He looked to see from where the gusts were originating and saw a small rectangular window less than a foot off of the ceiling that was opened at an outward angle. His weariness from the prior night had prevented him from noticing it. It was a way to possibly find out their exact locale, or at least narrow it down significantly. The problem was that he would have to rely on a description from Mike, who, from his position perched on the porcelain rail, was the only one who could see out.

"How's that arm feeling, Mikey?"

"It's better, I guess. It feels like someone is pouring warm water down the inside of it," he said, grinning.

"Do me a favor will ya', Mikey?"

"Okay."

"I want you to look out that window up there and tell me what you see."

Travis continued, "Do you see any buildings or road signs or anything like that?"

"Four million clouds," Mike replied.

A puzzled look came over Travis' face, and he looked at his older brother with furrowed brow.

"What does four million clouds mean, Mikey?"

Just before Mike could respond, the split and splintered door swung open.

Figg entered in his normal, cavalier manner.

"What are you doing up there, Mike?" Figg asked.

Travis interjected before Mike could answer.

"He's trying to get the feeling back in his arm for Christ's sake. Have you ever had your arm dangled over your head overnight? It's not exactly optimal for sleeping."

Figg was oblivious to the window. He was too concerned with expressing his giddiness over the brothers' hovel-like accommodations.

"Maybe next time we'll try to get you a couple of king-sized beds to sleep on. How's that sound, guys?"

He un-cuffed Travis' hands just long enough to re-cuff them behind him. He left Mike where he was.

"Let's go sit down and have a little talk, Travis."

"What about my brother? You gotta' let him come, too."

Travis had put a match close to the fuse again. But rather than getting in a tizzy, Figg simply slammed Travis into the wall across from the bathroom. He was getting tired of being treated like a rag doll. It reminded him of the time he spent living with his stepfather and the draconian nature of the three years at home before he left for the Marines.

When he uncoiled from the impact, he saw the inside of a large warehouse. It was truly massive. The only thing he could compare a contained space of such enormity to would be an airplane hangar. There must have been hundreds of stained windows lining the upper half of the walls. A number of them, like the tiles in the bathroom, were either partially or completely broken out. The bright sunlight coming in prevented him from being able to see out. There was a single poker table with foldable legs about twenty yards from the bathroom. It looked quite surreal, this single table, alone, in such a cavernous setting. The air was thick. The abundant rays of sunlight piercing through captured and revealed the clouds of sawdust and smaller particles floating in the air. The pollution was so prevalent and ubiquitous that the visibility throughout the warehouse was compromised. There was a strong smell of mildew that had been exacerbated by the precipitation overnight. Even though he could only see about thirty or forty yards in front of him, he surmised that they must have been almost a hundred yards from the front of the building.

Two flimsy metal chairs sat on either side of the table. Figg planted Travis into one of them and took the other, turned it backwards and straddled.

"Listen, Figg, before you say anything, my brother and I need somethin' to eat. We haven't eaten in almost twenty-four hours and we're both starving," Travis tried asserting himself.

"I've got some food on the way. I'm not gonna' let you starve, but don't act like you're in a position to demand anything." Figg leaned forward and folded his arms on the back of the chair resting his chin on his forearms. He sat there without saying a word. He stared at Travis for what seemed like a full minute. He moved the toothpick in his mouth from side to side but showed no discernable expression. The brute got up and walked over to a small metal stand that was against the wall. Travis hadn't noticed it. When he turned around, he held a white cloth, flat, over his palms. He laid it down on the table. Lying on the cloth was a spoon, a lighter, a syringe and a dime bag of heroin.

Travis' stomach dropped and his mind started spinning like a pinwheel. Across the table, Figg took notice of Travis' less than subtle reaction. He walked around and freed Travis' hands.

"What's wrong, Travis?"

The recovering addict swallowed a dry, empty gulp as he tried desperately to look anywhere but at the paraphernalia right in front of him. He had no idea what to do with his hands. He crossed his arms awkwardly and did his best to act unfazed.

"Does that make you uncomfortable?" Figg made obvious reference to the heroin. An excruciating silence followed. Figg was bathing in the torment taking place across the table from him. He watched with amusement as Travis sat, shifting from one posture to the next. Part of the recovering user wanted to light the dirt up and jab the long needle straight into his vein. The other part was resisting that urge with everything it could muster.

"I hope you're not waiting for me to say something," Travis managed to blurt out, breaking the hush.

"No, no, I'm not." Figg countered, as a devilish smile poured over his face.

I just want be sure you aren't interested in a quick fix. Ya know, just to relax and make you feel better. You look like you're hurting, and I thought I might try to help."

The two factions in Travis' head were jousting with little regard for the other. Finally, one faction came out victorious and Travis swept the materials clear off the table and sat back down with a look of fortitude and defiance. Figg's impish smile oozed even wider, from one ear to the other, and he began to laugh.

"You made a good choice, Travis, and so dramatic. Wow. It gave me chills. Now that we've gotten that outta' the way, what

I'd really like to talk about is a new offer that I hope you will strongly consider." Travis was naturally skeptical.

Figg applied the handcuffs yet again.

"Are you telling me that I have an option?" he asked.

"Good point. No, you don't."

"Why do I get the feeling that this offer is going to be on a playing field leaning heavily in your direction?" Travis asked.

"Now see, you've already got the wrong attitude about this whole thing, Travis. I think this venture will be beneficial to both of us." Figg spoke like a man with an ace up his sleeve.

"Well, maybe that's because when I chose not to accept the first offer, you, or one of your henchmen, tried to make me a part of the grill of a rather large truck." Travis said, referring to his brush with the maroon SUV.

"Oh, *that*. I heard you almost didn't get out of the way in time. That was just me being a little more persuasive. Believe me, Travis, if I wanted to kill you, you'd be on a cold steel gurney being poked and prodded right now." The fact that Travis knew he was right was a sobering notion.

He countered. "Are you going to sit there and make threats or are you going to get on with this offer?"

Figg, resting his head on his arms, started to manipulate his eyes wildly. His pupils darted from side to side, and then up and down, and again from side to side. If it hadn't been so bizarre, it would have been a most eerie sight indeed. Travis really didn't need any more evidence to know he was dealing with a teetering psychopath. The cop unevenly segued into a matter-of-fact tone.

"Since this is the biggest thing we've worked on together, what da' ya' say we raise the stakes a little bit?" Travis was wary of the words about to come from Figg's mouth.

"Now, your end of the deal entails the 'mark' that I gave to you the other day. This time, though, and I was really hoping it wouldn't come to this, but I'm afraid you're gonna' have to put a bullet in his brain for me." Figg's monotone lacked emotion.

Travis had prepared himself for such an "offer" but his arm and neck hair still stood on end when the words were spoken.

"Are you kidding me? I'm not gonna' kill anybody. There's no way you can make me do this." His reaction was involuntary.

Figg shook his head waiting for Travis to wrap up his predictable response.

"I knew that would be your initial reaction. But, you haven't even heard what I'm willing to do to help you make a rational, more sensible decision. See, my end of the deal is that, if you do exactly as you're told, then, I don't put a bullet in your brother's head."

Travis stood, hands cuffed behind him, and sent the table flying vis-à-vis a sweeping right kick and charged at Figg like a bull towards a red flag. A solid knee from Figg found his mid-section and his sally was cut short as quickly as it began. He fell to ground in a dusty heap. The distinct noise of a man gasping for air echoed throughout the naked warehouse. Figg stood over him, laughing, engaged in a bizarre sequence of tai-chi-like movements involving his arms and legs.

Travis had reacted without any clue as to what he was doing. And considering he lacked the use of his arms and hands, his reckless charge lacked prudence. He had lost whatever degree of control that he had been able to maintain up to that point. As he lay, doubled-over and gulping for air, Travis realized he had fallen near the bottom of his emotional trough. He had reached a point where there was almost no lower ground. To bottom-out further was a frightening thought. He also realized that, as low as he was, his only option was to get up and try to save the life of his brother. He thought about his Dad.

Travis struggled to his knees. His head was hanging as he continued to regulate his breathing. Figg had concluded his antics and kneeled down in front of the beaten young man. He grabbed Travis' cascading bangs and lifted his head.

"Have you gotten that out of your system? I hope you have, because I don't know how much more of this you can take and still be of service to me and Mike."

Travis had a look of concession on his face. Figg looked into his eyes for about ten seconds. He wanted to gain some satisfaction that Travis had, indeed, relented. He released Travis' hair and let his head sag.

"Can we sit down and try this again, Travis?" Figg reset the table and chairs to their original positions.

Travis managed to make it to his feet. He was in a tremendous amount of pain and still couldn't speak as a result of the blow to his gut. Nevertheless, he stumbled back to the table and delicately took a seat.

"Maybe you want that needle now?" Figg taunted him further.

Travis' hair covered his eyes and nose. He muttered, "Take off the cuffs."

"What did you say? I couldn't quite make that out," Figg replied.

Travis lifted his head.

"Take off the cuffs. You've got the fucking gun on your hip. Do you think I'm gonna' try to run? It would make it a helluva lot easier to cooperate if I could breath."

Figg placed his index finger under his nose pondering Travis' request.

"I guess you're right, kid. I mean where *are* you gonna' run?" he grinned.

"They were more for effect anyway."

Travis had no idea how much the restraints had affected his breathing and overall pain level. It was a relative feeling of comfort to be free of them.

It had been several minutes since Figg had been his usual wise-ass self, and he couldn't resist.

"Let me start by saying that I couldn't be happier to see you've agreed to work with me on this."

Travis decided to stop giving him the satisfaction of reacting to his psychoses.

"We are going to approach this in a somewhat unique way, Travis. We're gonna' approach this in segments. You will be given directives in, what I consider to be, very small increments. As you engage in these directives, I want you to have one ultimate objective. That objective is to take down the 'mark' when the time comes. Is that clear?"

Travis asked the question he had been dying to get off of his chest.

"Why don't you just do this yourself? Why do want to entrust something like this to me? I'm just a guy trying to take care of his brother and stay out of trouble."

Travis' inquiries visibly irked Figg.

"Wait a minute."

He put his index finger to his forehead and Travis prepared for yet another neurotic wise-crack.

"Does it say something on my forehead? Is there a word there? Seriously, Travis, do you see the word 'idiot' or 'moron' written here?"

Travis had already begun to come to terms with the fact that Figg knew about his past. He was about to find out how much.

"I've had my eyes on you for close to a year now. In my line of work it helps to know as much as I can about guys like you, Travis. Maybe one out of ten snitches actually ends up producing for me, but when you find that one, the one who is better, smarter and tougher than his situation, you have to keep that one in your hip pocket for future services. You know, heavier, more intense services. Do you think I would take a random kid off the street to do something like this? Give me a little credit, kiddo. Sure, I've used you for information in the past, but I really wanted to make sure that you were staying sober. Sober enough to squeeze the trigger if I needed you to. And now, I need you to."

Travis felt uncomfortable and exposed at how Figg had seemingly violated him without ever having any knowledge that it was taking place. And there was more to come.

"I knew there was a greater than zero chance you wouldn't take the assignment. I also knew that you would probably run. I was counting on it. I knew about your prowess with military ops, in particular with the rifle, but I had to see how you would conduct yourself under pressure, under a perceived crisis. I guess I wanted to know whether the junk you'd taken in the past had diminished your ability to think on your feet. And I must say, Travis, I don't believe it has. You've impressed me. And I've gotta' say, the leverage I'm gonna' use from your allegiance to your brother is just sweet, icing on the cake. You are the ideal candidate for this assignment. I think it's kind of ironic don't you? It will probably be your love for him that may end up getting him killed. Let's hope it doesn't come to that."

"You're a fucking psycho, you know that."

Travis had regained his breath just enough to bark out the insult. Figg took it as more of a compliment.

"You're just saying that," he feigned flattery.

"So there is no 'Vargas' is there?" Travis asked.

"Oh sure, there is a 'Vargas.' But he's not the man in the pictures you saw, and his name isn't Vargas. You'll find out who the real mark is when I decide that you need to know."

It was murky and a drab gray ruled the day. Raindrops fell as the officer leaned against the brick wall under the easement just outside the bar where they agreed to meet. He pulled a long drag from his cigarette. It was a bad neighborhood. Half the cars that lined the street were R.I.P., and the weeds scaled the chain-linked fences that surrounded the basketball courts. The rims had no nets and one of the backboards wilted at a ninety degree angle. Gangs lived here. Outsiders had better be cops or heavily armed, otherwise they were risking life and limb.

The second part of the meeting emerged from around the corner. He was tall, tattooed and tough enough to have gotten by in these types of neighborhoods for most of his life. The rain didn't have an affect one way or another on the speed of his stride. The ring through his nose was symbolic of the pissed off bull that resided within the young man. The sleeves on his black T-shirt were rolled up to accentuate the considerable muscle tone in his biceps and triceps. The cop held the door for him and they got out of the rain. They took a booth. The banger opened the dialogue.

"I hope you realize the chance I'm taking by showing up here."

"Why's that?" the cop asked.

"I'm seriously persona non grata around here these days for reasons I'm not gonna' get into with you. The only reason I showed is for my dad's sake."

"You'll be fine, kid." He didn't know whether he'd be fine or not, but he needed him to relax.

"Yeah, you're gonna' look out for me, huh," he said, drenched in cynicism.

They ordered a couple of beers and the cop began to try and tug some information from the boy.

"I hear you and your dad have tried to reestablish a relationship over the past couple a' months."

"Maybe, so what?" He was predictably defiant as the rainwater still rolled off his cleanly shaved head.

"Your dad may be in some trouble and I thought you might be able to shed some light on some of the things he may have said or done, you know, recently."

"Let me get this straight, cop, you brought me in here to narc on my father, just as we're starting to get along again. Is that a correct assumption?" The boy was well spoken in spite of his appearance and lack of education.

"Wait a minute, hold on. "Narc" is the wrong word here. I want to help protect your dad before he does something that the department won't be able to overlook. Do you understand that?"

"That's just a rosy, drawn out way of saying narc, man. And you know what else? I think you can have my beer. I don't drink with cops. I knew this was a waste a' time," the boy slid his glass mug across the table. The cop caught it before it landed in his lap.

The boy had a parting message.

"Good luck with your investigation officer," he meant the opposite.

"Sorry I couldn't help, but if there's one thing I won't do its rat, especially on my father," he headed for the door.

The cop dropped his head, frustrated by the dead end and second guessing his approach. He didn't expect the boy to spill his guts, but he hoped he might get something helpful.

Rat tat tat. Rat tat tat. Screeching tires peeled out. The cop ran out of the dark bar and saw a van speeding away and a tall, tattooed, tough kid slumped against the wet brick wall twenty feet from the bar's entrance. He rushed to the boy's side. He's soaked in blood from his chest to his knees. The holes in his chest are spewing blood like the Trevi fountains. The cop pulled him from against the wall and cradled his head while the boy's eyes rolled circularly, wildly. The cop ripped off his overcoat and stuffed it against the gaping, gushing holes and flesh, but it was like rearranging the deck chairs on the Titanic, futile. Blood trickled from both corners of the boy's mouth as his eyes stopped rolling, and he focused on the cop.

"You've killed me. And now, since I told my girl where and who I was meeting, she's gonna' tell my Pop, and he's gonna' kill you," he said, gargled. He managed to lift one corner of his mouth to smile and say,

"A dead man holding another dead man. Would you say that is more ironic or coincidental?"

And the boy was lifeless.-

Figg stood up and crossed his arms, smiling.

"I do have to admit, that thing at the bus station; that got a *little* sticky. You were never supposed to get that far. One of my guys wasn't where he was supposed to be and I really had to cover some ground to get to that bus before you guys left the city. Of course we're not going let anything like that happen again. That could have been a real problem."

"How did you find out about all this?" Travis asked, miffed at the turn of events.

"Find out about what?"

"My experience with special ops for starters."

"Like I said, Travis, I like to know who I've got on the payroll. And military records are easier to get than you might think."

Travis, robbed of his usual wit by Figg' verbal raping, searched for a modicum of indignation.

"I couldn't hit a beach ball if it was five feet in front of me anymore, Figg."

"If I believed that, we wouldn't be sitting here right now," Figg countered.

"We're gonna' have a good time. And maybe when this is all over we can have a barbeque together. You know, grill some burgers or somethin'," Figg continued.

"Don't count on that, asshole. And what do you mean *we're* going to have a good time."

"I'm gonna' be your chaperone, Travis. I want to make sure that everything goes smoothly. You can't blame me for that, can you?"

Travis decided the rhetoric didn't merit a response.

"What do ya' say we get going? Your first directive is to get up out of that chair and slowly exit this warehouse."

Travis did as he was told and began the lengthy walk toward the front of the building. Figg followed some six or seven yards behind him, gun drawn. Travis hadn't taken ten steps before he issued a caveat.

"If my brother is touched, in any way, I swear you'll wish you had chosen someone else for this little dog n' pony show."

"Shut up and walk," Figg was terse.

They stopped near the door.

"Put on this blindfold."

Figg reapplied the handcuffs and walked around to make sure the blindfold was in place and secure. He guided Travis gripping the back of his neck. They had almost reached the door when Travis heard the familiar voice of the driver.

"Where's the other one?"

"He's still in the john. Give him a little food," Figg replied.

"Right."

The driver held the door open and Figg guided Travis through.

Chapter Thirteen

Even iron will break when the pressure becomes too great.

THE THICK, HOT AIR SMACKED Travis across the face. It was bright enough that he could tell through the blindfold that there was little if any cloud cover this day. He could hear cars moving at high speeds not too far away. Figg moved him quickly to the door and stuffed him in the back seat of the car on the passenger side. It was a different vehicle than the one that had brought them there. The interior in this car was leather and it was more spacious.

It pulled away from the warehouse and began gathering speed.

"We never did get you anything to eat, did we? I bet you're thirsty too, aren't you?"

Travis, put off, and feeling very much the part of the victim, let Figg's bullshit go unrequited, even though it felt like rats were eating away at his stomach wall.

"My mistake kid, we'll take care of you ASAP. I promise." Travis was beginning to wonder if the evil that resided within the cop knew any depth at all.

He tilted his wrapped head and leaned it against the window. He was weak from not eating or drinking. The pain of his bruised side and broken fingers, though still present, had yielded somewhat to his need for food and water.

The volume of the acid rock playing on the radio grew louder and louder. A speaker blared directly behind Travis' right ear. Eventually the volume reached a level that shook his brain stem. The bass sounds rhythmically and unmercifully pounded his skeleton. He could barely make out the sounds of Figg slapping the steering wheel to the beat of the song as if he was enjoying it. Had he wised up to Travis' ability to navigate audibly, or was he just twisting the knife further?

This continued for what seemed like thirty minutes. In reality they had gone just a few miles before the car slowed and finally came to a jarring stop. When Figg took the keys out of the ignition and the music stopped, Travis' ears kept ringing. The ringing was so intense he couldn't hear Figg's latest caveat. The car door subsequently slammed shut and Travis found himself completely in the dark in both a literal and figurative sense. He couldn't see. He couldn't hear. And he had no idea where he was. For the first time throughout this entire ordeal, Travis' was genuinely scared. He was hardened. He was tough. He was resilient. But he was also human and had limits. As his fear peeked, he began to throw his body around in his seat. He slammed himself into the seat back and hurled his upper body into the car door. With his hands secured behind him, his right arm and humerus bone were taking the brunt of the impact. His already ailing head knocked hard against the window. He screamed at the top of his lungs for no other reason than to satisfy his psyche's dissatisfaction and torment. He had reached a fork in the road that offered a path to a dark dementia and another that led to keeping it together for Mike as well as his own sanity. He flailed until his muscles surrendered to the purest form of exhaustion. If Figg had offered the junk at that very moment, he would have succumbed. His body came to rest on its side lying across the backseat. His breathing was heavy. He was testing the waters of the sea that was a psychological Purgatory. Almost five minutes passed before Travis slowly brought his body back erect and into the seat. He sat in solitude. The ringing in his ears had subsided as he tried to gather his wits along with his limited bearings. Evidently, he had made a choice. The Purgatory's water was too hot for swimming. He thought about his Dad.

The driver side door opened and the aroma of greasy fast-food passed under his nose. He was whistling *Bluebird on My Shoulder*.

"Here we go." Figg said, as he sat down and waved the food in front of Travis' face.

He would lean toward the smell and Figg would pull it away, several times. His stomach had been growling like a pissed-off pit bull all morning. If his mouth could have produced it, saliva would have been spilling from his lips. Figg chuckled as he reached for the key to the handcuffs.

"Boy, oh boy, you sure look hungry, Travis." He was famished to the point that his need for food dictated what he heard and didn't hear.

Figg placed the carry-out tray on Travis' lap.

"Leave the blindfold on," he said.

That was fine by Travis. His hands were freed and he feverishly began to grope at the food resting on his legs. It was a hamburger. He clumsily shoveled morsel after morsel into his eager mouth. He mixed in a fistful of French fries that he had discovered while devouring the burger.

"Slow down, slow down. You'll choke." Figg chuckled again as he spoke.

"You wanna' wash that down, kid?"

Travis reached out, his hands moving erratically to receive the water Figg held. The liquid gold went to work immediately to relieve his sandy dehydration. It was a pathetic spectacle for sure. Naturally, Figg rather enjoyed the sight of a starving man blindly relaying life-sustaining nutrients down his throat. Travis continued to scarf the food like a termite taking to a pier and beam support.

The sizeable hamburger and bag of fries vanished in a heartbeat. Travis resisted the urge to ask for more knowing his request would be denied. He didn't want to give Figg the satisfaction.

"That looked like it hit the spot. Now come on, you know the drill." Figg moved to lock Travis' hands again and Travis obliged without resistance, turning to expose both wrists.

His face was covered with mustard, sesame seeds and fry crumbs.

"I don't suppose you're gonna' tell me where we're going are you?" Travis spoke for the first time since they had left the warehouse.

"Patience, Travis. You'll find out soon enough. I wouldn't worry about it. Besides, you've got bigger fish to fry. Remember what I said about keeping one objective in mind. I'll take care of the details." Figg was all business whenever he spoke of the "objective."

As they returned to the road, Travis, having finally been nourished, found his thoughts turning to Mike again. He wondered if he was all right. He could only pray that he wasn't being mistreated by the driver. The biggest fear weighing on his conscience was that Mike was afraid. He couldn't stand the visualization of Mike curled up on the floor of the slovenly, roach-infested bathroom wondering when he was going to be able to go "home." Travis wondered if he truly believed what he had said about everything being part of a pretend show. On top of all his concern was the frustrating realization that, while he knew Figg needed him for whatever he had planned, he probably didn't need him bad enough to keep from killing both him and Mike if he failed to cooperate. He had him over the proverbial "barrel". Travis' feelings of helplessness were running rampant.

He could tell now, from the sound of the cars whizzing around them, that they were on the freeway returning to the Beast. The windows were tinted, so there was no concern on Figg's part of someone spotting his captive. Once he had exited the freeway, taken a right, taken a left, veered to the right, executed a u-turn, Figg reached back and removed the blindfold from over Travis' eyes.

"There's no reason for you not to see where we are now." Figg broke the silence.

The sudden light blasted through the windshield marauding his deprived and sensitive eyes. He squinted badly as his sight slowly sharpened. He discovered they were in the financial district next to Thanksgiving Tower on Live Oak, heading west.

"Do you really have to keep these on?" Travis turned his head and tilted it in the direction of the handcuffs.

"I'm not going to do anything to risk my brother's life."

"Actually, Travis, I need you to keep those on for the place we're heading to right now. You'll understand in a second."

If Figg's goal was to thoroughly puzzle Travis, he had succeeded. True to his word, however, as he pulled the car to the curb and stopped, Travis got the clue. They were directly in front of the 44th precinct headquarters.

Chapter Fourteen

"...though I walk through the Valley of Death, I shall fear no evil for... God? ...is with me?"

FIGG REMOVED TRAVIS FROM THE car and proceeded across the street acting as if he were just bringing in another perp. The precinct doors sat atop a series of a dozen shallow steps. The area was teeming with navy blue uniforms and shiny badges. Travis felt like Daniel about to enter the lion's den. Figg nodded at a badge here and gave an obligatory "How's it goin'?" there. The cop and the snitch entered the lair. Even after his arrests for petty theft, he had never been to the 44th Headquarters. He had always met Figg at neutral, remote locales. Police officers were everywhere. They poured out of office doors and lined the booking counter like targets at a shooting gallery. Or, at least that's what it looked like to Travis.

"Sit here and keep your mouth closed." Figg seated him on a bench that hugged the wall several feet from booking.

Figg went to the counter and engaged in conversation with one of the desk jockeys. The exchange lasted only a few minutes. Figg turned and approached Travis with a blank look on his face.

"C'mon, kid. We're goin' upstairs".

"You don't even book people anymore?" Travis complained.

"For what? You haven't committed a crime…yet." Figg smiled like the devil as he gave Travis a strong shove forward.

They walked down the hallway to a door that opened to a stairway leading up. As the door closed behind them they were alone. Figg had some more "instructions" for Travis.

"I'm gonna' put you in a cell for little while. You would be wise to be as a quiet as a mouse while you're in here. I don't want anyone to hear you breathing. Do you understand?"

"Whatever." Travis' response was indifferent.

The door clanged behind him. He rubbed his wrists, sore from the restraints. Travis slowly panned the cage. He noticed but two others, one lying, the other sitting on opposite ends of a bench against the far wall. Not wanting to upset the balance, Travis chose a spot against the side caddy-corner to the wall and slid down the bars resting his arms upon his upright knees. Farthest from him was an older man who looked to be asleep on the bench. He was wearing an old, rag of an overcoat and torn blue jeans. The man's hair and beard were overgrown to the point that the skin of his face was barely visible. He was probably happy to be out of the elements, mild as they were, but was likely missing his good friends, whiskey and rum. His other cellmate sat erect with his back pressed firmly against the wall. The first thing Travis noticed about him was his build. He was finespun, bordering on sickly, and was an obviously user. He could tell that the man was about his own height and their hair color was similar. The man appeared to be in his forties. He noticed the man stealing quick glances at him out of the corner of his eye. Travis was not quite as subtle.

"What's your name?" He whispered.

The man turned to look, but didn't answer. Travis saw his face well for the first time. He asked again, "C'mon, man, I just wanna' know your name." Travis looked around to make sure Figg wasn't coming.

"Leave me alone. Don't talk to me, *alright*! Don't even *look* at me!"

Travis was taken aback by the man's less than impressive conversational skills. He pressed to find out why he was so objectionable.

"What's your problem? I just asked you your name."

"Listen to me very closely," the junkie said as he leaned in toward Travis. He looked up to ensure that they would not be overheard, save the passed out sod, much like Travis had a moment before. Consternation registered on the junkie's face.

"I saw who brought you in here. I'm in here on a bullshit dope charge, okay? I'll be outta' here in a few hours. I don't want to get involved with Figg or anyone who is associated with Figg. Got it?"

Somehow, Travis was not altogether surprised that the random dope-head was familiar with his blackmailer.

"You know Figg?" He popped off the inquiry quickly to keep the junkie's interest and his tongue.

The man seemed to drop his guard a little and demonstrated the lack of conviction that probably got him hooked on smack in the first place, and he continued.

"Yeah, and I bet you probably know what that guy is all about. I mean, that is one sick bastard. I saw him shoot a guy on the street one night for no reason. No damn reason at all! I was crouched down in an alley coming down from a fix, right? Across the street I saw Figg talking to one of those well-dressed, slick, pinky ring mob types, ya' know? -

"Hey, listen, Detective Figg. What can I say? The boss has decided to go with somebody else. That's it, end of discussion."

"I've been takin' care of you guys for five years now and Carbone doesn't even have the decency to come out here and do this himself?" Figg asked, angrily.

"This guy costs half as much as you do and from what I hear, he's a helluva lot more effective, too," the goon responded.

"More effective than me? You say he's more effective than me? I gotta' tell ya', I find that extremely hard to believe. Not only is that hard to believe, I would go so far as to say it's impossible."

"What the hell are you talkin' about, Figg. Why's that impossible?" the goon asked.

"Unless he's the devil, himself," Figg replied.

"Alright, now you're losin' me, pal, this conversation is over. I'm goin' back inside. You fucked up and that's it. So go on your way while you still can, got it?" The goon fiddled with his gold pinky ring and turned to reenter the back door of the restaurant.

Figg drew his gun and held it at his side.

"The Angel of Death doesn't make mistakes!" Figg said with a raspy snarl as he cocked the hammer on his pistol.

The goon heard the noise and turned back around, puzzled by the peculiar comment. Very coldly and very calmly, the unbalanced police officer raised his weapon and deposited a single bullet between the goon's eyes just as he had started to reach for his own gun.–

"He fell like a house of cards. Figg walked back to his car as if nothing had happened and drove off. Can you believe that? '*The Angel of Death doesn't make mistakes.*' What the hell is that?" the junkie exclaimed. "It's like he thinks he on some sort of unholy crusade against anyone and anything that doesn't fit into his warped existence. How does a lunatic like that get a badge? It scares the living shit outta' me. And this was only about a month ago!" The junkie put a closed fist to his mouth and scanned the area surrounding the cell realizing he had already said too much.

Travis, still somehow a little shaken by the detailed account of Figg's brutal nature, acted as if he wasn't.

"Yeah, the guy is definitely a monster."

The junkie nodded, concurring.

"Then you'll pardon me if I don't care to make chitchat with one of his prisoners."

And with that, he stood and walked several feet away from Travis and took a seat next to the drunk.

Meanwhile, Travis started to mull over what he had just heard. Was this a Mafia related thing? It was difficult to say. Figg had his hand in so many bags that he could be at odds with any number of groups or individuals. He didn't want to make an assumption in an effort to prevent any surprises. It was mandatory that he try and stay on a relatively even keel.

There was a clock on the wall across from the cell, and Travis saw between the bars that it was almost three o'clock in the afternoon. He guessed he had been sitting there for nearly an hour and a half. A few more scofflaws had joined the fray over that time. Just as he was about to doze off, the mechanical roller tracks of the cell door grumbled and Figg barked,

"Travis, get up."

He did as he was told and made his way into the waiting hand of a visibly irritated Figg. He was abusing Travis even more than usual as they moved toward the stairwell. The cuffs were applied quickly and carelessly. They were painfully tight.

"What the hell, Figg? Loosen these cuffs man. There cutting off my circulation."

Not only did Figg not respond, he pushed him harder than he ever had before and Travis' legs and feet sped underneath him to keep him from falling to the ground, face first.

"What's your problem? Take it easy!" Travis remarked, indignantly.

Figg was in one of his moods.

"Don't say another damn word," he huffed.

It was obvious that something had set Figg off. The cause was anybody's guess. Travis knew that trying to guess what moves the insane into a tizzy was a Sisyphean endeavor. He hazarded a few guesses anyway. He was thinking that it was likely one of two things. Either he hadn't found what he was looking for, or, he *had* found what he was looking for and it had left a really bitter taste in his mouth.

As they approached the stairwell door, Travis was rightfully concerned about being thrown down the stairs. What was to stop Figg, in a rage, from pushing the immobilized prisoner down the stairs? Figg used Travis' stomach to push down the door bar and open it. They came to the precipitous peek of the staircase that consisted of ten steps. It would be long, hard fall. He closed his eyes and braced for the worst.

"Watch your step."

"What?"

"Watch your step and go down the stairs."

Travis was surprised and relieved.

"What? Did you think I was going to push you?"

Figg had thrown Travis for another giant loop with a vintage mood swing.

"It crossed my mind," Travis admitted.

"What good would you be to me with a broken neck?"

Even with the ulterior motive, Travis was surprised at Figg's ability to harness his emotions with the flick of a switch. They proceeded down the steps, entered the first floor hallway and weaved their way to the oversized front doors.

"It's time to make a dry run." Travis assumed Figg was referring to a process of familiarizing him to the area in which the hit was going to take place. Travis played stupid to see what else he could get out of him.

"A dry run?"

"Yes, a dry run. Or I guess what you guys call 'scouting' the area. I'm going to show you exactly how you will proceed, step by step, to execute your objective. I want everything to be precise, down to the second. There will only be a small window of opportunity for you to take out your target."

Travis continued needling.

"Where are you gonna' get a rifle. I hope you know that I'm gonna' need a weapon that meets my specifications."

Figg became predictably irritated.

"Don't worry about that right now. The purpose of this is so you can get the timing down, nothing else."

"It's just that I haven't fired a single round in almost four years, that's all. And I won't be comfortable with a run-of-the-mill

SWAT rifle." Every time Travis opened his mouth, it just pissed off Figg further.

"*Shut up*, you little shit. *Shut the hell up*! I said don't worry about that right now. Don't say another damn word about it. Got it?"

"Fine."

They took a left turn at Harwood Street and traveled about a mile before Figg pulled over to the south side curb and stopped the car.

"Look across the street," he said.

Travis saw a large four-story parking garage that overlooked a street level lot. The street lot sat between the garage and a very ordinary looking stone building that stood a little higher than the garage.

"You're target is going to exit that building at approximately five fifteen tomorrow afternoon." Figg pointed to stone structure.

"He will walk to his car. It will be parked in a reserved parking spot in the adjacent lot. The spot is numbered fifty-two. Do you understand?"

"Yeah."

"Now get out and walk over to the lot and find the spot I just described." Figg unlocked the cuffs.

Travis was taken aback.

"You want me to walk over there into a lot full of cars right now," he asked.

"Yes, Travis, that's what I want. Do it, now."

Travis got out of the car and made his way across Harwood. He stopped short of the lot entrance and looked around to make sure no one was watching him. With great caution, he proceeded into the paved area. Every space was occupied so he had to walk between the cars to get a look at the reserved numbers. He came to spot number fifty-two. It was a high-end luxury sedan that looked almost new. It was white with gold trim and the Texas plate read "TYH-008". Travis was in the process of committing the plate number to memory when he felt someone tapping on his shoulder. He momentarily froze. Long enough to hear the words, "What the hell do you think your doing?"

He turned slowly to see a short, stocky figure wearing a white shirt and a reflective orange vest over it. It was the lot attendant. Travis bought some time to come up with something.

"You scared the hell outta' me. Boy oh boy, you really did sneak up on me, didn't you?" Travis could tell the attendant took his comparatively meaningless job quite seriously.

"I asked you, what the hell do you think you're doing?"

"Ya' know, I thought this lot cut through and I was just trying to save a little time on my way across town." He thought that was decent spur-of-the-moment bullshit.

"No it doesn't cut through and why were you looking at this car right here." He pointed to the mark's car.

"Uh, well, I dropped a quarter and was just picking it up, that's all." Travis turned his back and reached down to pick up the phantom coin.

The attendant gave Travis his best skeptical dog eye.

"I'll just head back out of here and take the long way around. No big deal, right?"

"Don't let me see you here again unless you're parking a car."

"Yes sir, you got it. I'm gone,…thank you."

Travis walked backwards with a gracious hand extended in the direction of the attendant accompanied by a few more empty platitudes. He quickly turned taking speedy, gaping strides as he departed the lot, walked back across the street and returned the front seat of the car. He was surprised to be greeted by a laughing Figg.

"What the hell are you laughing at?"

"Did you have a problem with reflector man over there?" he asked, making reference the attendant's orange vest.

"I don't know what's so funny. If you want this thing to go off without a hitch, things like what just happened over there are a most unwelcome occurrence."

"Hey, watch your tone, Travis."

"What tone?" Travis asked, sensing another bi-polar episode.

"Like I don't know what I'm doing. I know exactly what's goin' on here. Don't tell me what you think is goin' on here. Because what you think is goin' on here doesn't mean a damn thing." Again, Figg snapped off a most uneven segue.

"In the trunk there's a janitor's jumpsuit. Put it on in the back seat."

Travis hesitated as if he was trying to put two and two together.

"Get out."

He did as he was told. Figg popped the trunk. Inside was a plain black jumpsuit, a dark baseball cap and a pair of thin leather gloves. There was also a black flak-jacket. Travis got into the backseat and began putting on the jumpsuit. Figg put the car in reverse and came to a stop in front of an older brick building. It was probably built around nineteen thirty or so and was seven stories high. The building had a great deal of character. Most of the color had been washed off of the red brick exterior. It was lined with symmetrical, individually spaced single windows. Each of which had a custard yellow paint on the sills and frames that had been tastefully reapplied over the years. Travis finished squeezing into the garb.

"Alright. Why the hell did I put this stuff on?" he asked, put out.

"Get out and walk in front of the car. I want to make sure everything fits properly and looks right." Figg replied.

"Are you serious?"

Figg turned around. The tightening of his jaw made the need for words unnecessary. Travis got out and posed for him. He extended his arms and engaged in a slow, three-sixty degree circle. Satisfied, Figg waved him back into the car, cuffs ready.

"There will be a small crowd in front of this building when you approach from the west side at five o'clock. Four officers, including myself, will be working the disturbance. I'll be on the end closest to you when you approach the building. We will enter the building together. *Do not hesitate*! Do you understand? You will *not* hesitate. I want you to carry yourself like you know exactly what you're doing.

"I will get you past any obstacles around the front desk. Take the east stairwell to the fifth floor and proceed to room number 505. The door will be unlocked and the office will be completely empty except for the weapon and a pair of binoculars to survey the area with. You will have two windows to choose from to take the shot."

Travis searched for holes in Figg' plan. One thing was obvious: Why would he need binoculars if he already had a scope mounted on the rifle?

But Travis didn't say anything. Instead, he redirected Figg's focus.

"How the hell am I gonna get a rifle up there?"

"There you go again, underestimating the amount of thought I've put into this. This is the last time I'm gonna' say this; you worry about one thing and one thing only. That is executing your objective."

Travis revealed how he had processed the information he had just been given.

"Let me see if I've got this right," he was smarmy. "You're going to call in a bomb threat to evacuate the building. While you're working the evacuation process, the hit will be taking place simultaneously providing you with the air tight alibi of dozens of witnesses, not to mention several other cops. Meanwhile, you will be able to supervise my work and make sure that nothing goes wrong. Tell me when I miss something."

"See, that's why I had to have you on this assignment, kid. You're just too damn smart for your own good."

Travis asked a question he already knew the answer to. "So what happens to me?"

"Leave everything, including the outfit, in the room and take the east stairwell all the way down to the garage level. Once you're in the lot beneath the building, you'll be able to get out using the exit ramp on the east side of the building"

"And then what?" Travis asked.

"Make your way to the corner of Akard and Main. I'll pick you up there as soon as I verify that the mark is dead."

Travis was, at the very least, suspicious.

"Will you have enough time to decide how you're going to kill me by then?"

Figg laughed.

"Don't think like that, Travis. Why are you so negative? Try being a little more optimistic. It does wonders for the soul."

Chapter Fifteen

You can get slapped around, or...

FIGG TURNED WEST ONTO PACIFIC as he pulled the cell phone from his coat pocket. He pushed the redial button and cradled the phone to his ear. He waited briefly for the pick-up.

"Wheeler."

That was it. He spoke one word, "wheeler", and hung up.

"What the hell is wheeler?" Travis asked.

"Don't you mean *who* is Wheeler?" Figg said, playfully.

"Okay, who is Wheeler?" Travis played back.

"He was almost a very important man. And he's also the fella' who just kept your brother alive for at least one more hour."

Travis felt a combination of anger and confusion. "Wheeler?"

He couldn't even begin to ascertain the significance.

"I guess this is the first time we've been together at the top of an hour, Travis."

Travis immediately looked at the digital radio clock. It read five o'clock.

"If my friend doesn't get that call every hour, with the right name, your brother will get to meet his Maker."

Figg was happy with himself. He loved boasting about what he understood to be his own impeccable plan.

"It's just a little insurance. In case you decide to get brave or stupid or something like that. Besides, you can never be too cautious with an ex-Marine, can you?"

Travis shook his head at the absurdity of Figg' comment.

"Well, you could at least loosen these cuffs and put them on in front. Even an ex-Marine can't do a whole lot without the use of his hands."

Figg dismissed Travis' request.

"We'll worry about that later."

"Let's talk about something of greater importance," Figg changed the subject.

"I'm going to give you the opportunity to tell me what you're going to need in order to carry out your objective."

Travis had been wondering when he would finally broach the subject. But he objected to the way Figg phrased it as *his* objective.

"Don't you mean *your* objective?" He replied with a moderate amount of indignation.

"Now, see, we can't afford to have you thinking like that, Travis."

Figg grabbed the wheel with his left hand and threw his right hand landing it squarely on Travis' chin. His head careened off of the window. He was getting used to the type of pain that accompanied such a blow.

"Dammit, Figg!"

"I hate having to do that, Travis. Please stop making me do that."

He paused for a few seconds. "Now, let's try this again. Would you like to tell me what you will need?"

Travis was still working his lower mandible, shifting it from side to side making sure there was no lasting injury.

"I'll need an AR-15 rifle with a bipod and an eight-inch silencer. You do want me to be as quiet as possible, don't you?"

Figg gave him an unappreciative sneer. Travis continued.

"I'll need a telescope that will have to be specially mounted to meet my specifications. I will need .55 grain .223 caliber bullets with high muscle velocity. And I will need a light trigger pull." Travis rattled off a sniper's vernacular.

As much as Figg tried to appear halfway knowledgeable, Travis knew he'd have to repeat it. He didn't dare say anything, though, as his face would undoubtedly pay the price. All the while, the name, Wheeler, kept rolling around in his thoughts as he searched for its relevance. He could find none. He would have to pay close attention to the next check-in at 6:00 P.M. and hope he would be close enough to Figg to hear the keyword. If he was ever going to be able to escape, he would have to decipher whatever system Figg had employed. It was unlikely that he would be able to get to Mike in less than an hour. He paid close attention to the time as they continued heading west. It was 5:20 P.M. as they rolled into a one star motel about ten miles southwest of Dallas in the suburb of Duncanville. It was becoming clear that nothing else was going to happen on this day. He was not looking forward to another night locked to the toilet and was hoping Figg would imprison him in a more humane fashion.

Figg knotted the blindfold and went inside to make arrangements for a room. Travis was mulling how he would keep Figg around until six o'clock. He knew that once they got to the room and he was locked up that Figg wouldn't stay very long, if at all. He had to come up with some sort of stall tactic for at least twenty minutes. Figg pulled Travis out of the car, yanked the blindfold from his head, and they walked down the jagged breezeway to the last door of the dilapidated, one-story, strip motel.

As Figg opened the door and pushed him through, Travis was not surprised to be met with the stale stench of body odor, mildew and cheap beer. He immediately looked for some sort of a clock in the room. On the nightstand rested an old clock radio. It was the kind that was about twice as big as it needed to be and had hands and a dial instead of a digital readout. It was the type of early seventies clock that no one would even want to steal, which was probably the only reason it was still there. It read five thirty-eight. There were two single beds with teal covered spreads on either side of the night stand. The pillows were lumpy and looked most uncomfortable. The headboards had initials, unsavory phrases and phone numbers in case you were "looking for a good time" carved into them. The T.V. had to be twenty years old and rested on a flimsy metal stand. The carpeting was cream colored shag that had been pulled up in several spots and worn through in others. The stain blotches were challenging the clean spots for majority coverage of the room. The brown wallpaper wilted off the walls at several areas around the crown molding. The bathroom was on the other side of the room and the door was halfway ajar.

"If you leave me in that bathroom all night, I swear my body will be so out of whack, I won't be able to hold a rifle, much less get off an accurate shot."

"What makes you think I was gonna' do that?" Figg asked as he closed the door behind them.

"Gee, I don't know." Travis laid on some sarcasm of his own.

Figg shoved Travis and he fell onto the bed farthest from the door. Staring up at the ceiling, Travis decided how he would vamp for the next twenty-five minutes until the six o'clock call-in. He sat up.

"What happened to you?" he asked in an overly inquisitive tone.

"What the hell do you mean, *what happened to me*?" Figg shot back.

"You know, what turned you against everything? What turned you into such a nihilist. You obviously have a problem with just about everybody, and I was just wondering if there was some reason for it."

"Nihilist? That sounds like one of your little dime-store philosophy words. Did you just learn that?" Figg was crabbed that Travis would use a word he didn't know.

"What the hell is *nihilist*?"

"It just means that you don't believe in any order, spiritually or otherwise, kind of like an anarchist," Travis imparted his limited knowledge of Nietzsche's principles upon Figg.

"Well, that doesn't sound like a very nice thing," Figg was flip.

"Are you gonna' answer the question?"

"Maybe I'm just wired that way, Travis. How 'bout that?"

"No, that's a cop-out. It has to be something more than that." Travis continued probing to see if he could press a button.

"What the hell are you doing?" Figg asked

"I'm not doing anything. I'm just curious about what happens to people like you to make them void of any goodness or compassion."

"I haven't killed your maggot-ass yet. If that isn't goodness or compassion, I don't know what is." Figg dropped into the chair that sat in the corner next to the window at the front of the room. He placed his hands over his eyes and ran his fingers through his wiry black hair. He appeared to be fighting fatigue. Travis was encouraged. He saw it as a chink in the armor.

"Was there ever a time where you weren't the way you are now?" Travis wanted to keep stalling.

Figg sat with his head back, resting it on the chair back. He didn't respond immediately. Instead, he started humming a tune, softly at first, and then louder. Travis quickly recognized the song.

It was *Happy Birthday.* The humming became louder and louder and finally reached a crescendo as Figg belted out "HAPPY BIRTHDAY TO ME!!"

"Did you know today is my birthday, Travis?"

"No, I didn't know that, Figg. If I had, I would have baked you a cake. But I just haven't had much time to do much cooking the last few days, ya' know."

"That's funny, kid. I'm glad to see you still have a sense of humor about all this," he smiled.

"You asked me why I am the way I am, Travis?"

"Yes."

"Are you sure you really wanna know?"

Figg unbuttoned the cuff on the right wrist of his long sleeve shirt. He carefully rolled it back to reveal a series of dark red and purple scars. They ran from his inner forearm all the way up his arm to his inner bicep. The scars ran parallel two by two in a pattern that was obviously methodical in nature.

"These are all birthday presents from dear old Dad. He started when I was six, but he had to make up for the first five that he had missed. So on my sixth birthday he used my arm here as an ashtray a half-a-dozen times. I was lucky. I passed out after the third. He never missed another one after that. Did you know many kids that were terrified of their birthday, Travis?"

Travis wouldn't allow himself to feel pity for Figg, though it was hard to hide his disgust at the sight of scars.

"But, if you'll count 'em up here." Figg started to count the marks.

"…ten, twelve, fourteen. It stops at fourteen. You know why it stops at fourteen? Because I killed the son-of-a-bitch the night before my fifteenth birthday."

Travis wasn't quite prepared for Figg to spill his guts and was careful not to interject for fear that he might clam up.

"He had guzzled his usual twelve pack of cheap beer and passed out in his recliner in front of the T.V. I didn't know where my mother was, which was pretty much standard. My Pop kept a .12 gage shotgun under his bed. I had been preparing for this night for a long time. So, when it was time, I went and got the gun. It felt huge in my hands, and it was heavy. I had never fired a gun before, and I was as nervous as long-tailed cat in a roomful of rocking chairs. I grabbed two shells from his dresser drawer and loaded it. You might find this hard to believe, Travis, but I was shaking like a leaf as I walked down the hallway toward the den where he was passed out. I never had any second thoughts about what I was going to do, but when you're about to fill your own father full of lead, it's difficult to act with too much certainty. As I got to the T.V. room, I actually tip-toed around the recliner, trying to avoid the aluminum cans that were scattered all over the floor.

It smelt like a brewery. I'll never forget the odor that was in the room that night, it was his odor. I stood ten feet in front of him and raised the shotgun, the barrel aimed right between his eyes. His head slumped and drool was running out of the corner of his mouth. Can you guess what I did then, Travis? Go ahead, take a guess."

"I have no idea, Figg. What did you do?"

Travis found himself drawn into Figg's recount.

"I said, "Wake up, Pop, wake up."

"He slowly came to and lifted his head. I gave him a few seconds to gather himself. I wanted him to see exactly what was about to happen. As soon as he was able to focus, he wiped the saliva from his chin. There was no fear in eyes. He looked at me with his usual cold, icy glare. I don't think he ever really thought I would do it. But then he said something that I'll never forget. He looked at me and said, "Well, it's about damn time, you little shit."

"What do you think he meant by that Travis?"

Figg's question came across as rhetorical, but also as one that had plagued him from the time he heard it until here, this very second.

"That's when I pulled the trigger. The next thing I know, it's raining blood and chair stuffing. Once everything cleared, I saw the seat overturned and on top of him. That's the last thing I remember. The court, and all of its officers, took one look at the scars on my arm, along with the assortment of bruises all over my body, and figured I had been through enough already. They just sent me to one of those homes and ordered the standard psychiatric follow-ups. And as for my mother, well, you're guess is as good as mine. I'd imagine that she's long gone. From all my Pop told me about her, she couldn't have lived very long with all the stuff she was into. And that's just the tip of the iceberg, kid."

Figg sat silent for a moment with a sidetracked, contemplative gaze. Abruptly, he returned to his soliloquy.

"So you wanna' know if there is any goodness in me? You wanna' know if there's even a heart pumping in my chest? You wanna' know if I'm a bad man? If I'm just plain evil incarnate? Maybe so. But remember, without evil, where's the good? If evil didn't exist, no one would know what goodness was, would they? Without darkness, there would be no light, and all that blah, blah, blah. It's all part of that yin yang thing, ya' know. The world needs people like me to keep the balance. So you think you're life has been tough, kid? Well, you'll have to pardon me if don't have a whole lot of sympathy."

Travis was wishing he had come up with another line of questioning, although the autobiographical diatribe did explain quite a bit. Suddenly, he realized he hadn't checked the time. He looked at the clock. He saw one minute after six. Panic set in as he looked to see if Figg was preparing to make the check-in call. What he saw was Figg slowly rolling his sleeve down.

"Aren't you gonna' make the call?"

"Make what call?"

"Dammit, Figg, don't fuck around. Make the call."

Figg patted the pockets on his chest area of his coat as if he was trying to find his cellular phone.

"Have you seen my phone, Travis?"

"Don't do this, Figg. Make the call now!"

"I'm serious. I think I left my phone in the car, or, maybe it's up at the front desk."

"This isn't funny you son-of-a–bitch. Its three minutes after the hour. If you let something happen to Mike," Travis couldn't continue.

His anxiety started to affect his breathing. He began to hyper-ventilate and fell to his knees at the feet of an amused and jovial Figg.

"Travis, Travis, relax, kid. I made a call while you were in the car. Notification won't be necessary for a little while. Your brother is fine…for now."

Travis fell onto his side wheezing as his oxygen intake gradually returned to normal. Figg snickered a little as he stepped over Travis and walked into the bathroom closing the door behind him. For the first time, Travis started fantasizing about all the ways he could kill Figg. He imagined the most painful thing he could inflict on his body. He wanted to torture the corrupt cop to the point where he would beg him to for death. Travis had reached the point where he couldn't abhor another human being anymore than he did Figg at that moment. He sat up, still trying to regulate his breathing, and managed to shimmy his ass over to the wall and leaned against it. Figg appeared from the washroom wiping his face with water. He walked to the table and began to put his coat on.

"Hey, if you're gonna' leave, couldn't you at least cuff me to the bedpost or something?" Travis requested.

Figg stuck out his lower lip feigning sympathy.

"Is little marine boy uncomfortable?" He used baby-speak.

"I swear if there's one thing that has surprised me about you, Travis, is just how big a pussy you actually are."

Nevertheless, he went to the bedpost and shook it violently to test its worthiness. Content, he accommodated Travis. Then he took the phone that was on the nightstand and pulled the cord from the jack in the wall and placed it on the other bed far from Travis' reach.

"Bring some food when you come back."

"We'll see." Figg said as he left the motel room.

Travis lay on the bed closest to the door with his left hand connected to the bedpost. He surveyed the room to see if Figg had overlooked anything that he could use to somehow free himself. After a few minutes of searching he realized he hadn't. The post was surprisingly solid considering its age and seemingly crude craftsmanship. At first glance, there didn't appear to be any instruments within reach that would contribute to an escape attempt. Satisfied that he was not going anywhere, he laid, spread eagle on the bed and his body got an opportunity to cross-examine him. His head, chest, side and hand were all stating their case for relief. Of all those with an argument, Travis felt his head had the best case. It was still sore from the butt of the driver's gun the day before.

In his aching head, he went over a variety of scenarios of how he could engage Figg and try and get away when he returned. He knew that the check-in calls had been suspended for now, but could resume at any time. Once it was evident to Figg that something was amiss, it could mean one stroke of the redial button. Travis had few opportunities available to him. He was going to have to wait until the calls resumed, pray that he could decipher the series of names Figg was using and continue the calls. All of this would be moot if he couldn't, somehow, incapacitate his kidnapper. He had been suppressing the thought of carrying out the 'hit' all along. He knew that once it was complete, he would be a dead man walking. There was no way he would live and be allowed to tell any tales. In fact, he couldn't remember Figg even offering clemency of any kind. Once he caught them on the bus just before they were to be free and clear, he and Mike were already morgue meat. They had been issued a death sentence. It was more motivation than he needed to find some way out. He continued to mull over his limited options. Exhausted, and unable to think very clearly, he decided he would resume exploring his chances after a few hours sleep.

I walk to the corner to see what's going on. Standing there is my brother Mikey, and several of the other kids from the neighborhood. I notice that they are all holding baseball cards, fanned out like poker hands. The other kids are laughing at Mike.

"What's goin' on here?" I ask.

"Oh, not much," The tall kid says, barely able to contain himself he's carrying on so much.

"You're genius brother here just traded me a rookie Pete Rose card for some guy no one's ever heard of," he says.

"Is this true, Mikey? Did he trade you this for your Pete Rose rookie card?"

"Yep, he did, I think it's a fair swap don't you, Trav? Why is everyone laughing?" Mike asks. "He told me they were really good players and it would be an even swap."

I look at the other kid.

"Why did you tell him it was an even swap when you knew it wasn't? You cheated my brother," I say.

"Give him the card back and get the fuck outta' here," I'm so pissed off, I can barely see straight.

"You know what they say, buddy, 'let the buyer beware'," he issues the caveat with a smart-ass grin that showed the massive gap between his two front teeth.

"All deals are final," he continues.

I crack my knuckles as I form a fist with my righhand. He is still laughing at Mikey, as are the others.

"All deals are final, huh?" I say. Before he can even answer, I launch my right fist toward his face. I feel his cheek bone for only a split-second as my hand recoils off of his mug. The kid's baseball cards go flying and he's falling backwards onto the ground. His head makes a popping noise as it bounces off the pavement. Blood is all over his face and forehead. He doesn't move once he's on the ground. The other kids stop laughing and scatter like cockroaches. I start sifting through the cards that are lying on the sidewalk until I find Mikey's Pete Rose rookie card. I hand it back to him. The kid is unconscious and his head is hanging backwards off the curb.

"Don't ever fuck with my brother again," I say, even though I know he can't hear me-.

Chapter Sixteen

Sometimes, your future *<u>is</u>* *what you make of it.*

TRAVIS AWOKE TO THE BLARING voices of two people engaged in a melodramatic war of words just outside his door. It sounded like a wife unsatisfied with her husband's commitment to their wedding vows. The voices were muffled as they entered the room next door. He roused and reached across the bed, scrambling with his available hand to turn the clock into view. It was nine o'clock and Figg hadn't returned.

As he rubbed his face and eyes he experienced an epiphany of sorts. Something clicked and the eureka of the moment slapped him flush in the face. Travis realized how he would attempt to free himself. He was going to take the leap. It was time to take a chance. His adrenaline began to flow in a positive direction and his nerves stood on end. He didn't even realize that he was sitting straight up and his foot was tapping at the rate of a hummingbird's heartbeat. Now, he could hardly wait for Figg to come back.

"Wait a minute." Travis told himself.

He had to maintain a level head.

"*You've got to calm down. Just settle down.*"

He took several deep breaths. He was going to have to contain himself if he was going to pull this off. Added to that was the fact that he had no idea how long Figg would be gone. He began to take the necessary steps to prepare for his escape attempt.

"Pace yourself, you could be in for a wait". He told himself.

And that is exactly what he got. The ten, eleven and midnight hours passed in what seemed like three days. He had been ready for Figg' return for almost two hours now. He fought to maintain his mental readiness. As each minute passed, bits of adrenaline were replaced with a growing sense of ennui.

Finally, at twelve fifty-seven, he heard footsteps approaching the other side of the door. There was a fiddle of the doorknob, and it was unlocked. The door swept open. Travis again engaged in some inner-dialogue.

"Calm yourself. Don't tip anything off. Calm yourself…"

Figg closed the door behind him and immediately made his way to the restroom.

"Can't sleep, huh?" he said as he turned the faucet on and splashed his face with water. He came back into view drying his face with a washcloth. He pulled the cell phone from his pocket pressed a button and held it to his ear.

"Give me a name. Give me name." Travis' inner dialogue implored.

"Arthur."

He had a second name. Figg had delivered it with a bow on top. Travis was having trouble keeping a stoic exterior.

"It's time to be movin' on, kid."

Figg walked over to release the cuffs in order to relock his hands behind him. Travis exploded off the bed at an arms length from his captor. In his hand was the large clock radio that he had worked for nearly an hour to unplug and tuck under one of the lumpy pillows. With his good hand, he started the three-pound clock radio in a wide, circular path bound for Figg' skull.

Before Figg even realized an object was coming toward him, now with great velocity, Travis ferociously slammed the makeshift weapon into the side of Figg' head. His glassless frames shattered on impact. The blow was so intense that his body flew forward onto the bed. The anti-Christ's body lay motionless, face down across the narrow twin.

Travis stood over him, his heart about to leap out of his ribcage and onto the floor. The surge of adrenaline that came with the blow had left him a little dazed. A full minute passed before he realized that his hand was still locked to the bedpost. The adrenaline had bested his logic. The keys had been thrown onto the floor by the end of the bed during the assault. He stretched his leg and desperately tried to use his foot as a rake to bring the keys closer. They were a foot out of reach.

"Oh, c'mon, Travis, you idiot," he chided himself.

He stood there, almost hysterical, as his mind was going a million miles a second trying to think of a way to extend his reach. He pulled Figg over and onto his back. There was a grisly gash to his head. Travis began undoing Figg' belt and started to pull on the buckle. The dead- weight of Figg's unconscious body made it difficult to slide the belt through the loops on his pants. Travis placed his leg on Figg's hip and pushed against it for leverage as he pulled. The belt released suddenly, and Travis fell backward into the wall. He held the end opposite the buckle and began trying to drape it across the keys to pull them closer. On his fourth attempt, he was successful. Travis quickly grabbed them and unlocked himself. He rushed to the other side of the bed and got a closer look at the bludgeoning that had created a crimson drip to the side of Figg's skull. He checked his pulse to make sure he hadn't killed him. There was the pressure of a heartbeat. He zealously began to search his body for the phone and the keys to both the car and the room, plus his .40 SW. Once that was done, he completed the "turning of the tables" by cuffing Figg to the same bedpost. Travis stopped at the door and turned around. He gave the room a short, but thorough, once over. He thought he would be content to just get the hell out of there and start looking for Mike, but something was keeping him there. He couldn't leave the room. He looked at the weapon he was now holding in his right hand and he looked at Figg, helpless, sprawled across the bed. He could put an end to the miserable monster's life right now. Travis found himself slowly approaching Figg and standing over his head, which hung over the edge of the bed, bloodied. He put the gun's barrel between his eyes. All he could think about was how all his problems would go away if he pulled that trigger. He had come to a fork in the road and it was time to choose. Kill him, and take his chances finding Mike-or not. He loved his brother with every fiber of his being, but life would be so much easier buying just the one ticket to Memphis and starting over. He pulled Figg's wallet from his coat pocket. He opened it revealing a stack of bills inside a half-an-inch thick. They were mostly twenties. There had to be $500 dollars inside. The temptation was palpable. How realistic was it to think he could take care of Mike and they would grow old together? That they would end up spending their days on a rustic, shaded porch rocking into a comfortable breeze and drinking mint juleps. The flip-side was that he would be starting over alone. Snapping back to the moment, he pressed the barrel harder between the devil's eyes, his finger tickling the trigger ready to twitch and change his life forever. His mind raced and he flexed his jaw muscles as the tension in his face and throughout his body grew stronger and stronger. Strangely, and quite unexpectedly, Travis had an epiphany come over him at that very moment, and the clarity of it was unmistakable. He realized that almost everything bad in his life had come from the bullet. His parent's double-suicide had led to him joining the Corps, and losing touch with Mike. His physical prowess with a rifle had led to an emotional collapse, drug addiction and life on the streets. Bullets were the root of everything that had gone wrong in his life. And it most certainly didn't seem like they could be the remedy either. He thought about Dad.

He pulled the gun back to his side and exhaled like he had been holding in all the air in the room. Every muscle in Travis' body cut loose tension as his body recoiled into a relaxed state. He shook his head and cussed himself for even entertaining the idea of abandoning Mike. He wasn't going to take the easy way out. His brother was far too important to him. He took a single twenty from Figg's wallet, stuffed it into his pocket and tossed the billfold onto Figg's chest. Satisfied, he left Figg unconscious on the flea bag motel room bed, took the car, and fled the scene.

Chapter Seventeen

Good friends can be hard to find.

"WHEELER", "ARTHUR". THE NAMES ROLLED around in his mind like the last two ping pong balls in a hopper. He could only hope that the pair of names would be enough to establish a third. He would need it in forty-six minutes. He put his foot to the pedal and sped his way east, back to the Beast. His initial thoughts were that he names had something to do with law enforcement. Maybe a list of the most recent officers killed in the line of duty, or recipients of some kind of commendation. Then again, it might be a million different things. He remembered Figg telling him that the names were of men that were "almost very important men." That was all he had to go on. With his options still somewhat limited, he decided he would give Cubby the first crack at it. His knowledge was ubiquitous, and he might be able to assign some kind of meaning to the names. The needle on the speedometer fluttered between eighty and eighty-five as Travis was almost halfway to the Lamar exit off of Interstate 30. He weaved in and out of the few, law-abiding cars and trucks that were out after midnight on a weekday. Every second was precious. The annoying voices of the dispatcher and responding officers came almost non-stop over the scanner sitting in the front seat. Travis fiddled with the knobs until he found the power switch. He looked up just in time to veer onto the R.L Thorton merge. The exit loop was less than a mile away now. The lit bulbs of the sphere atop Reunion Tower were blinking in a circular pattern directly in front of him. Travis accelerated to speeds nearing one-hundred miles per hour as he closed in on the Beast. He now had twenty-nine minutes to come up with the keyword. He took the loop at forty miles an hour and upped it to seventy as he crossed over I-35. It was one-thirty in the morning and he was headed to the underbelly of the Convention Center to see if he could find the proverbial "needle in a hay stack."

He sped through the only traffic light between him and Cubby and skidded to a halt across the street from the heaping piles of junk that surrounded Cubby and Monte's living quarters. The time was one forty-one a.m.

He slammed the car door shut and dashed across the street.

"Cubby, ...Cub!"

Cubby liked to cover himself in the pile of fiberglass insulation, tattered blankets and old bed sheets.

"Cubby, are you under there? Cub, talk to me!"

Travis feverishly began pulling blankets and pieces of insulation from the heap. Almost halfway through, he uncovered someone. Monte unleashed sharp, piercing screams that echoed off the walls of the rail stop.

"Monte, Monte, calm down, calm down. I'm not going to hurt you."

He could barely hear himself talk as Monte continued to shriek like an eleven year-old girl. Travis decided to ignore the screams as it was obvious that words were of no use and Cubby was nowhere to be found. He returned to the car in a panic. He knew that Cubby never ventured very far from his "home," so he started to drive north, very slowly, hoping to spot his friend. Travis drove at close to fifteen miles-per hour with all four of the windows rolled down.

"Cubby!...Cubby, are you out there?"

Travis continued to shout his friend's name, but there was no answer. He decided to go to the fast-food restaurant around the block. Cubby would sometimes hang out at Mickey's late at night and eat his chicken sandwiches with fries. He parked the car in the spot nearest the door and irrupted into the greasy spoon. In the far corner booth a man lay asleep with a tray full of garbage on the table in front of him. It was Cubby. Travis jutted over and around the formation of tables and whacked Cubby on the arm as he slid into the booth across from him.

"Get off me, you bastards!"

Cubby response was sleep or dream induced.

"Cubby, it's alright. It's me, Travis."

He furrowed his brow at Travis, still not quite awake.

"Travis? You look like hell. What happened to you? What are you doin' here? What time is it?"

"That's not important right now. I need you to think for me. I have a question that I need you to answer for me. Can you do that?"

"Son, that depends on the question. What's gotten into you anyway? You're goin' a mile a minute."

"Wheeler and Arthur, Wheeler…Arthur. Do those names mean anything to you?"

"Wheeler and Arthur?" Cubby repeated vexingly. "That's not a question, Travis. That's some kind of brain teaser. Is that all you have?"

Travis, discouraged, searched his mind for something more. Then, it popped into his head.

-"wheeler."

That was it. He spoke one word, "wheeler," and hung up.

"What the hell is wheeler?" Travis asked.

"Don't you mean who is Wheeler?" Figg said playfully.

"Okay, who is Wheeler?" Travis played back.

"He was almost a very important man. And he's also the fella' who just kept your brother alive for at least one more hour."-

Travis looked up at Cubby.

"Yes, there is something else. They were both 'almost very important men'."

'Almost very important men,' Cubby repeated.

Travis stared at Cubby while he engaged in the thinker's pose.

"I don't have much time, Cub, does that ring a bell or not?"

"Hold on, Travis. Give me a second."

Travis was squirming in his seat with every passing second He was beginning to feel the grief of having killed his brother already setting in.

"Well, in the history circles I used to walk around in, the most famous 'almost important men' were United States Vice Presidents. Now, I can't place those names exactly, but they sure do sound 'almost very presidential' to me.

"You think they may be Vice Presidents?" Travis clamored with new found hope.

"I wouldn't mortgage my spot by the rail on it, but I'm pretty sure, Trav."

"Oh my God! I love you like a father, Cub. So who was after Arthur on the list?"

Cubby responded with a look that pared Travis' gathering optimism.

"That, I don't know, Trav. What the hell's goin' on here anyway? You're mixed up with that cop, aren't you? I knew when I didn't see you for a couple of days something was wrong. Where's Mike? Is he okay?"

Travis shook his head and buried his eyes and forehead in the palms of his hands.

"He's got him."

"Dammit, Travis, what did I tell you? *What did I tell you!"*

"Cubby, please, I don't have time for a lecture right now. If I don't get the next name in fifteen minutes, he's gonna' kill him."

"Oh no, Travis, Oh no! What have you done?"

Travis just sat there, head buried in his hands. Cubby looked around in a panic. He stood up because he could no longer sit. He paced up and down the aisle.

"Come on, there's one thing left to try," he said.

Travis could only muster a half-hearted show of enthusiasm.

"I've got a car right out here," He said.

"Where are we going, Cub?"

"To see if a certain savant might have something buried in his card catalog that might help."

Travis' mood took an upswing. It was actually a viable option that Monte might be keeping the list he so desperately needed in his head.

Travis fish-tailed the turn back onto Lamar and sped back to Cubby's hole hoping to find Monte again. He snuck a peek at the digital clock which now read one forty-seven. As he skidded into a stop the car ran up onto the curb and bounced to a halt. Travis hastily got out of the car. Cubby took a little longer.

"Monte, its Cub." He said as he approached the rag heap. Monte's head rose from beneath the debris like a prairie dog peering out if its hole, and he turned to see the two nearing.

"Hey, kid. I was hoping you could help me and Travis out with somethin'. What do ya' say? Can you help us out?"

Monte didn't respond, but Cubby knew that he had gotten his attention.

"Think *real* hard for me, okay. Do you have a list of United States Vice Presidents in your head somewhere? Have you memorized that list?"

Monte lowered his head. He pulled his knees to his chin. He was silent. Travis feared the worst. Cubby pressed the savant.

"Now think, Monte, this is very important, Vice Presidents."

They waited for what seemed like several minutes of silence. Suddenly Monte began enumerating.

"Washington, Adams, Jefferson, Monroe, Madison,…" He rattled off a list of Presidents.

"No, not Presidents, Monte, *Vice* Presidents. I know it's a little harder. Try again." Cubby said.

You could see Monte searching through the trivial archives in his brain as the helter-skelter that was his pathology bounced around in his brain. He twitched and mumbled as he disregarded and filtered out bits of data trying to narrow the scope of his search. Almost ten minutes had elapsed and Travis was starting to get that ugly feeling in the pit of his stomach again. He took a seat on the curb and pulled at the hanging locks of hair draped over his face. Cubby still stood over Monte, waiting.

"Adams, Jefferson, Burr, Clinton, Gerry, Tompkins, Calhoun, Calhoun…"

Travis lifted his head to the sweet melody of Monte's rambling recollection of the Vice Presidents. Cubby couldn't contain his excitement.

"There you go, boy! There you go! Travis get over here, he's got it! He's doing it!"

Monte spoke very quickly, so they both listened intently for the keywords "Wheeler" and "Arthur".

"Breckinridge, Hamlin, Johnson, Colfax, Wilson, Wheeler, Arthur…"

Their ears perked up.

"Hendricks, Morton, Stevenson, Hobart, Roosevelt…"

"Wait a minute slow down, Monte, slow down. What was that after Roosevelt?"

Monte was speaking at an incredibly fast pace.

"I lost you after Hobart."

Travis pleaded with him to slow down, but the train had already left the station. Monte continued on, tuning out any and all outside dialogue. Travis was running out of time. He was able to make out the next five names that would last him at least until the Dallas Public Library opened at seven a.m. that morning where he could get an extended list. He pulled the cell phone from his tattered jeans pocket and hit the redial button. He walked a good distance away from the prattling savant to make the call. All he had to do was say the name "Hendricks" into the phone in a low, monotone voice. Butterflies fluttered wildly in his gut. He heard the other end pick up.

"Yes," the driver said.

"Hendricks."

Travis waited for approval. Instead, the driver hung up. He assumed that was par for the course and wasn't terribly concerned. He turned to see Cubby looking at his prized gold timepiece.

"One fifty-seven. Thank the Lord, our God Almighty! One fifty-seven."

He laughed with relief and Travis couldn't hold back a wide smile of his own. Monte was still going and had gotten to Nixon and the vice-presidents of the nineteen sixties. Travis walked right up to Monte and gave him a bear hug. Monte squeaked several more names as he having the wind squeezed out of him.

"You have no idea what you've done for me, Monte," he said.

He turned to Cubby who was smiling wide. Travis walked up to him as well. He pulled Cub's hand to him, pulled the twenty from his pocket and slapped it square in his palm.

"You guys go get a steak."

"Lordy, Lordy, Trav. You don't have to do this."

Travis was already back in the car, closing the door behind him.

There was no way of knowing how many names, or hours, he would need to find Mike. But one thing he knew for sure was that he had been given new life.

Chapter Eighteen

For every angel, there exists a demon.

TRAVIS PULLED INTO AN ALLEY five blocks down. The myopic nature of the last hour left Travis at a loss for what he was going to do next. He had to regroup. He took a few minutes to gather his thoughts. He looked around the car to see if Figg had left anything that might be of use. There was no telling how long he would have to use the vehicle, so he didn't waste any time. He didn't find anything of substance inside. There might be something in the trunk. He hit the remote trunk unlock and it popped open. Sitting squarely in the middle of the oversized trunk was a long, black, padded gun cover. Travis reached into the trunk and unzipped the cover to find an immaculate, brand new AR-15 rifle. The side pouches contained a mountable scope, a bipod connection, an eight-inch silencer and just two .223 caliber bullets. Figg had gotten everything that Travis told him he would need. There was even a four-foot strap in the bag that Travis hadn't even mentioned to him. He pulled the weapon from its cover and brought the stock to his shoulder.

A wave of emotions came over him.

"The target is in the strike zone!"

"Pull the trigger, Hawk 1! Pull the god damn trigger!"

The sniper was shaking so badly that he couldn't keep the crosshair anywhere on the target's body. He fired a shot that shattered the small, stone gargoyle sculpture next to the target. The mark scrambled to cover.

"What the hell is going on up there, Hawk 1? Talk to me, Hawk 1. Give me your status, over. Do you copy?"

The sniper pulled back his weapon and crouched down behind his cover. Drops of sweat lined his brow and upper lip. He closed his eyes. His breathing was short and uneven. He slowly drew the radio to his face.

"Target not hit. I repeat, target not hit."-

Travis tossed the rifle back into the trunk of the car. It felt like he had been jabbed with a thousand needles all over his body. He put both hands to either temple, and bent over at the waist. The cracked, gravelly pavement was spinning beneath him, and he felt as if he might vomit. He stumbled over to the nearby brick wall and collapsed onto it. He stood there leaning against the structure with his head hanging and eyes closed tightly. The mere touch of the AR-15 had triggered a vivid flashback from his previous life. It was clear that he had not come to terms with that very significant part of his past. The trauma was as great now as it was the day he was discharged. Travis slowly allowed the episode to pass and collected himself. He walked back to the open trunk and prepared to slam it shut when he took notice of a folder that was lying underneath the rifle. He grabbed it and got back into the car so he could look at it under direct light. Its contents were revealing. The folder contained a plethora of photos with some documents mixed in. Almost all of the photos were taken without the subject's knowledge. The most disturbing aspect of the collection was that many of them were of Travis. They showed him carrying out several aspects of a daily routine. The shots included Travis at "home" with Mike, sitting with Cubby, and a street side exchange with Espinosa. Also included were a number of pictures of a man Travis didn't recognize. Immediately jumping off the print was the fact that the man was completely bald. Not a shaven bald, but a cue ball, gleaming bald. Lard oozed over his belt to the extent that you could easily see the white inner-lining of his pant waist. His chin was fully submerged in the fat that had aggressively replaced his jaw line. Compounding the problem was the fact that he stood somewhere around 5'5" or 5'6". He had left obesity on the side of the road miles ago. He was white, appeared to be in his forties and wore metal rimmed, round spectacles. There were several snapshots of the man on the streets involved in conversation and eating. He continued leafing through the black and whites, with nothing catching his eye. The last photo in the stack, however, confirmed what Travis had suspected since he began looking through the pictures. It showed the man about to step off the curb and cross the street. On the very left, lower edge of the frame he made out the rear of a white sedan with gold trim. The last three digits of the plate were "008." He was the mark. Travis closed the folder and set it down in the front seat.

For the first time since this mess started, Travis felt confident. He had taken control of the situation and had a sense of empowerment. With the information in the folder he had given himself some room to maneuver. He drove to the end of the alley and sat there, weighing his options. Though he still didn't know Mike's exact location, he could narrow it down to a few square miles southeast of downtown. He could also keep him alive for what he hoped would be long enough to find him. It didn't make sense to look until daybreak. First, he would head back to the plain, stone building on Harwood and find out a little more about the man Figg wanted dead, which wouldn't be possible for three or four hours, so he had some time to kill. Once he had resigned himself to the fact, he felt the growling of his stomach. He realized that he hadn't eaten in over twelve hours. He dug around in his pockets and was surprised to find an extra five dollar bill remaining from the hundred, or so, dollars Figg had given him the morning before. A small part of him wished he had kept the twenty that he gave to Cubby and Monte. But for a homeless man, it was enough to eat like a king. Time to find a twenty-four hour diner.

Chapter Nineteen

Meanwhile, back in the regular world...

HE COULDN'T AFFORD TO NOD OFF. He had to be awake at the top of every hour.

"Hello."

"Morton."

Travis flipped the cell phone and placed on the table. It was three in the morning and he had found a greasy spoon down in Deep Ellum.

"What can I get for you?"

A middle-aged woman with big hair readied her pad and pen.

"Gimme the ham and cheese omelet."

"You got it."

Her face had makeup caked on in layers, and huge, golden hula-hoop earrings hung from her ears.

"Can you add onions to that?"

"I don't see why not."

"And a cup of coffee, black."

"Okay"

"Thanks."

"Sure, honey."

The big-haired, big-accessorized waitress jotted down the order and relayed it to the kitchen window. There were eight or ten other-worlders in the diner. Most of them were twenty-something's who had too much to drink after a night of gallivanting from club to club on Elm Street. There was a police officer sitting at the counter caddy-cornered to Travis, who had snagged a booth. The cop was nursing his own caffeine fix. He smiled as he mixed with the big-haired server. It was only a patrolman taking a break from the late shift, but Travis always got nervous whenever a flat-hat was in the immediate vicinity. He looked over in the direction of Travis. He looked away from the officer and looked down. A minute or so later, a cup of coffee slid right under his nose. He saw his face in the rippling reflection of the java. His face was so dirty he could see the smudges under his eyes. He took a sip and looked around for the washroom. It was on the other end of the restaurant from where the cop was sitting. He decided he needed to splash some water on his face. He closed the door behind him and turned to see a filthy, malnourished, emaciated figure in the mirror. He leaned over the sink and looked closely at his reflection. With his index fingers, he parted the hair that was hanging down over his eyes and tucked it behind his ears. Violet bags bulged from underneath his bloodshot eyes. There was still some dried blood up around his hairline. Everything was accentuated by the overall pallidity of his skin. He reached for the handle and the cold water began to flow from the faucet. A small eddy collected around the drain. He cupped his hands and scooped some water to his face. He pulled several paper towels from the dispenser and began to dry. Travis gazed at his himself in the mirror, yet again, and became introspective. He had shelved the self pity and the lamentation over his current predicament long ago. He wondered if Figg was still alive or if he had died as a result of the blow he had delivered to his head. He wanted to believe that Figg would remain unconscious well into the next day, handcuffed to the bed in that sleazy motel room.

His inner voice was interrupted by a knock at door. He didn't respond, hoping that whoever it was would leave. There was a second knock. This one was harder than the last. Travis felt compelled to respond.

"There's somebody in here!" he said.

"Open the door," A deep voice demanded.

A furrowed look came over Travis' face as he was paralyzed with fear and confusion.

"Wait just a minute," he stalled.

"Please, open the door, quick!"

He didn't know what to make of the persistent man at the door. He slowly moved for the handle and turned it. The press-button lock popped out and the door was forcefully pushed open. It sent Travis reeling into the wall. Everything was a blur for a split-second. When he looked up he saw one of the bar-hoppers cradling the porcelain receptacle. His head was buried up to his neck. The liquor had gotten the better of the local college frat-rat. It sounded as if the young man was literally puking his internal organs out.

"Next time, mix in a glass of water," Travis was irritated with the boozer.

He left the heaving sod to his business and quickly walked back to see an ample ham, cheese and onion omelet at his seat. The events he had just witnessed would likely quash the appetites of most, but needle in Travis' stomach was well below "E", and he dove at the platter with an unleashed voracity, barely leaving time to savor the forkfuls of egg. Travis' appreciation for food had grown immeasurably now that he was only eating one meal a day.

"I'd say you were pretty hungry, huh?" The waitress returned to see the platter licked to a glisten.

"I just hadn't eaten in awhile, but it was good."

"Can I get you a danish or somethin' like that?"

"No thanks."

"You want your check, honey?"

"Sure, I guess so."

She took the platter and left Travis with his cup of coffee. He looked at his watch and noticed that he had spent close to a half an hour at the diner. The jolt from the caffeine had his thoughts racing again. As it stood, he was going to have to get to the Dallas Public Library when it opened at seven o'clock in order to get a full supply of "almost very important men." He had only been able to gather enough names from Monte's list to last him until eleven a.m. He would need to secure at least seven more names and would probably go ahead and get the rest of the list. It meant he had close to four hours to kill before he could resume *his* objective, which was to find his brother, no matter what the cost. The thought of waiting around idly while the whereabouts of Figg were not one hundred percent certain was very unsettling. Could the god-awful motel that he left him in have a maid service that would check in on the room? Had he regained consciousness and summoned help? What if when he came to and been found? What if he had reported the car stolen? Travis stopped thinking about the negative possibilities and tried to remain focused on what he had to do. He desperately wanted to begin his search, but without knowing how long it might take, he had to allow for more time than he currently had. There had to be something he could do before the library opened. The one thing that kept coming to mind was to return to the plain stone building on Harwood Street. Maybe his mark was an early riser and would be willing to talk. Talk about why a psychopath like Figg was intent that this be his last day on earth. Or, at the very least, he could find out who or what he worked for.

Travis looked at the check for the omelet and coffee. He had budgeted very carefully so that he wouldn't order more than he could pay for, but he had been so ravenous and was terrible at math and figuring sales tax. He hoped he hadn't over-ordered, especially now that there was a lawman nearby. His five dollars just barely covered the meal. He scampered out of the establishment, embarrassed by the seven-cent tip he left for the waitress. In the midst of the most bizarre imbroglio of his entire life, he was still concerned over a tip for a broken-down waitress working in an all night diner.

Chapter Twenty

Welcome to the party.

THE FOUR O'CLOCK AND FIVE O'CLOCK hours passed without incident as Travis lay in wait about a half-block down from the mark's building. The sunrise started to peek over the horizon about five forty-five, and the bluish tint of the inevitable dawn slowly replaced the darkness. The commotion of a new day began to gather strength over the next twenty minutes. Wispy steam escaped through the ventilated manholes and was rudely beaten and broken up by the swirling downtown winds. A few workaholics were starting to claim parking spots in the naked lots. He saw the over-zealous attendant from the day before taking his post, blowing on a cup of hot coffee, a newspaper under his arm. Travis put the car in drive and crept a little closer not wanting to let the white sedan sneak by him.

There was a tap on the window. Travis jumped as he turned to see who it was. As long as he didn't see a navy blue shirt and a badge everything would be fine. What he saw was the sagging, wrinkled and weathered face of an old man. He was wearing a plain, white, button down, collared short-sleeve shirt and an apron rested over his left shoulder. Travis rolled down the window.

"Can I help you?" Travis led off.

"You can't park here," the old man said.

Travis looked around and noticed he was parked in front of a coffee shop. "Hank's Coffee Shop" to be exact.

"Well, you must be Hank then."

Travis tried, in vein, to be engaging.

"Yeah, I'm Hank, and you gotta' move this car."

"Come on, Hank, there's nobody around. Cut me some slack. What do ya' say?"

"Unless you're coming in for some coffee, boy, move this car or I'll call the cops," he continued. "The damn cops are letting the parking get out of control around here!"

"Whoa, whoa, hang on there, old-timer. I'll move, okay?"

"These two spots are for customers only." The cantankerous, white haired proprietor spread his twig-like arms and gestured with his hands to indicate the area in front of his store.

"Okay then, sorry about that."

Travis looked back and forth between the man and the entrance to the parking lot. He moved the car forward, and he was almost directly adjacent to the mark's building before the curt senior citizen stopped shooing him away in the rear view mirror.

"What an ass." Travis mumbled to himself softly.

It was almost six o'clock, so Travis pulled the list from his jacket pocket and prepared to buy another hour. A few minutes passed.

"Stevenson." Travis was very non-distinctive and monotone in his delivery.

He hung up and began an inner dialogue,

"What an odd list for someone like Figg to use—Vice Presidents. Granted, it is very obscure. I daresay no one outside of presidential historians and scholars like Cub would be able to name a sequence of Vice Presidents from the nineteenth century. Was it really necessary, though? I mean, it would have been a long shot, at best, to escape him and get to Mike anyway. It's almost as if he's playing a little game for his own amusement. Figg seems to be locked into a bizarre, sociopath combination of very serious, substantive thought and very superficial, non-germane, almost playful thought."

The more he thought about it, the less sense it made. That was water under the bridge now, though, because whatever the case was, these were the ground rules within which he had to operate.

At six thirty-two, a white sedan with gold trim turned the corner onto Harwood. Travis ducked out of sight as license plate "TYH-008" pulled into the parking lot, stopping briefly at the booth to obtain his ticket.

It was time for Travis to employ the stealth that he had used so successfully as both a transient and a former special operations marine. He tucked the pistol into the back of his jeans and the folder full of photos down the front. He crawled across the front seat so he could exit on the side of the car away from the lot. He then stood and walked quickly along the opposite curb until the structure blocked the attendant's line of vision. He ran across the street and positioned himself against the wall of the mark's building about halfway between the lot and the entrance. He slouched a little and lifted one foot, placing the sole of his shoe against the wall. Hopefully, if he looked relaxed, then the mark would be less apprehensive as he approached. Within seconds, the bald, fat man emerged from around the corner, briefcase in hand. He plodded toward Travis. He was walking with his head down and had yet to notice him. Once he got to within five yards, he finally caught Travis out of the corner of his eye. He looked at

Travis and greeted him with a non-descript nod. He suspected nothing. Travis nodded back as he conspicuously reached for his weapon. The mark passed and Travis pivoted off of the wall as if he and the mark were tied together at the waist. He pressed the barrel of the .40 SW into his lower back.

"Keep your hands away from your body and keep walking," Travis demanded.

He felt the fat man's body become stiff as a board. The mark stumbled slightly before regaining his stride.

"Take it easy, take it easy." The man said as he lifted his arms outward.

"*Don't make it so obvious, put your arms down.*" Travis barked.

The mark brought his arms in from a ninety degree angle to about forty-five degrees.

"You don't want to do this. You have no idea who I am," the mark warned.

"You're right. I don't know who you are. That's why I'm here. Keep walking."

Travis pulled the barrel back to conceal it. He trailed so closely that he had to synchronize his steps with the mark's to prevent getting their feet and legs tangled.

"Do you want money? You can have all I've got. My wallet is in my back left pocket."

"Shut up. Turn left at the end of the block."

"You have no idea what you're getting yourself into." The fat man's voice cracked with fear.

"I know a lot more than you think, pal."

"I'm a cop." The mark said as Travis shoved him with his free hand so he would move faster.

They turned the corner and continued walking until they had reached cover behind several large, discarded cardboard boxes and two industrial-sized garbage dumpsters. They were alone. Travis patted him down and found the sidearm in shouldered holster. He confiscated it, placing it on the cardboard box to his immediate right.

"I'm not gonna' hurt you, okay. I just want to ask you a few questions." Travis tried to soothe the mark.

"You do know that there are twenty Internal Affairs officers in this building right here don't you?" The fat man's question was more of a warning.

"Internal Affairs, huh? And I assume that would include you?"

"You're damn right!"

"Well, then, maybe you can tell me why a homicide detective by the name of Figg is trying to blackmail me into putting a bullet through your brain."

The fat man's face grew pale and he looked for somewhere to sit down.

It was probably the wrong thing to say to someone who had just had a gun taken out of his back, but Travis wanted to move beyond the I've-got-a-badge-and-you-don't attitude he was sensing from the mark.

"He's after me now?" The mark acted as if he had no idea.

"Yes he is. Do you want to tell me why?"

"I guess I should've expected it." He replied, taking his glasses off and wiping his brow with the handkerchief from the breast pocket of his brown pin-striped suit.

"I've been trying to build a case on Detective Figg for several months now and only recently had enough information to confront him. He blames me for his son's death now as well, even though I didn't have anything to do with it." The fat man was in denial that he was even indirectly involved in the shooting.

Travis was taken aback by the revelation.

"I didn't even know he had a son," he responded.

"Yeah, some illegitimate bastard about eighteen or nineteen. He was killed in a drive-by shooting a few weeks ago."

At that moment everything became crystal clear in Travis' mind, and he imparted his knowledge on the mark.

"Lemme' guess. You contacted him two or three days ago about what you had, didn't you?"

"That's right," the mark replied.

"And yesterday, you met with him at the 44th to present him with what you had? Say, around three-thirty in the afternoon?"

The mark was surprised at Travis' wealth of information.

"How do you know all this?" he asked.

"That's not important right now. What is important is that if I don't end your investigation, vis-à-vis ending you, he's gonna' kill my little brother whom he's holding hostage. I'm trying to avoid having to do that, so I would really appreciate your cooperation."

"How do I know you're telling the truth? I mean, look at you. You can't be more than twenty-five years old. From the look of you, I'm assuming you're either a user or homeless, maybe both."

"You don't get it, do you? Maybe Figg was right about all you Internal Affairs guys being idiots."

Travis pulled the folder from his jeans front. He handed it to the mark.

"Think whatever you want about me, asshole, but I think those pictures tell the story. I found them in the trunk of Figg's car just a few hours ago."

The fat man deliberately examined the collection. A look of disbelief came over him as the reality of the situation began to present itself.

"My God! I knew that he had crossed the line a long time ago, but I had no idea how far he's actually gone off the deep end."

Travis enlightened him.

"He'll do whatever it takes to destroy you and whatever it is that you have on him. And now that you've told me about his son, you better believe he has a one-track mind right now. It is absolutely vital that you not get I.A. or anyone else involved in this. Just lay low for at least twenty-four hours until it plays itself out."

The mark didn't appreciate being instructed by his would-be assassin, but reluctantly acquiesced to him.

"Where is he now?" asked the fat man.

"I left him out cold at a motel in Duncanville earlier this morning. I'm not sure if he's still there. I *do* know that he's not gonna' be very happy when he comes to," Travis answered.

"Are you sure there isn't anything I can do to help?"

"No. Stay away from all the places you normally are on a day-to-day basis. Leave your car here. Take a cab to wherever you think you'll be safe. Give me a number where I can reach you if I need to."

The mark gave him a business card and penned in his personal cell-phone number on the back.

"How can I reach *you*?" he asked Travis.

"You can't."

That wasn't what he wanted to hear.

"You put a gun to my back and tell me you've been assigned to kill me and all I'm supposed to do is walk away and keep my mouth shut?" he complained.

"That's right. I realize it's not an ideal situation, but, if you stop and think about it, it's a helluva lot better than the alternative. Wouldn't you say?" Travis' rebuttal successfully disarmed the malcontent.

"Fine." The fat man ceded once again.

"At least tell me how it was suppose to go down," he pined.

Travis didn't see any harm in telling him.

"In the parking lot, a single head shot, medium range, quickly, cleanly."

Hearing the cold and calculated modus operandi for his own murder was brutally sobering. He dabbed away at his moist, wrinkly forehead with his kerchief.

"Just like that, huh?' he said.

"Just like that," Travis echoed.

Travis handed the butt end of the fat man's gun to him and he tucked it away. As the mark made his way back out to the street, Travis was left with the impression that despite everything he had told the mark, that he wouldn't let it go without getting involved in some fashion. It was a chance he would have to take. He didn't have time to worry about it. He needed to buy more time so he could begin his search for Mike. The Dallas Public Library would be open in twenty minutes where he would get a complete list of the vice presidents.

Chapter Twenty One

Even the best laid plans…

TRAVIS PACED OUTSIDE THE LIBRARY'S revolving glass door, anxiously awaiting its opening. He still had two names remaining from the list Monte had given him and would use one of them in a few minutes. He could see the time on the bank sign down the street as it flashed 6:56 a.m. and 59 degrees. The morning rush hour was hitting full stride. A small group of bookworms had gathered, waiting along with Travis for entry. He pressed his face against the glass panel to the side of the revolving door. He didn't see any library staff preparing to open the door. The bank marquee flashed 6:59. Travis walked a short distance away from the gathering and made the call. When he turned around, he saw people disappearing one-by-one into the building. Travis joined as the caboose of the medium-length line. Once inside, the first order of business was to execute a computer search with the keywords "vice" and "presidents." He frequented the library many times in the past to read-up on political theory and kill time, so he knew how to go about finding materials in the most efficient manner. The search indicated the material he sought was on the third floor.

Travis ran to the south side stairwell and flew up the steps, taking them two and sometimes three at a time. He slung-shot himself around the stair posts and was up three flights in about fifteen seconds, then sprinted down the long hallway to the west wing of the building. He couldn't help but notice that the materials he was looking for were about as far away from the library entrance as possible. No matter. He finally came upon the aisle with the book he needed. He pulled it from the shelf and hastily began leafing through it until he found his holy grail, the page enumerating all the 'almost very important men' ever to grace the 'almost very important office' of the vice presidency. Travis looked around before ripping the page from the binding of the encyclopedia volume. Haphazardly, he folded it and stuffed it into his pocket.

He swung through the door and noticed that getting the names had taken him just nine minutes. He made his way through the maze created by the gridlocked, backed up traffic and got into his illegally parked car. Travis' adrenaline began to pump a little harder. He was finally prepared to begin the search for his little brother. He put the keys in the ignition and started to turn the keys over.

The cell phone in his jacket pocket rang.

"What the hell!" was his involuntary and startled verbal response. Travis couldn't possibly be any more stunned than he was by the phone's chime. He was so shocked he couldn't even place the "William Tell's Overture" ring. He pulled the phone out and gazed at it helplessly. It chorused relentlessly.

Physically, he couldn't move his arms and hands to answer. It stopped after the fourth chorus. He couldn't look away from the phone. After another ten seconds, the maddening "Overture" began again. Travis tried to snap out of the hypnotic-like trance he had fallen into. In his head, he began to ask himself a series of question in the span of a few seconds.

"How many people have this number?"

"Who are the people that have this number?"

"Is it the driver?"

"Is it *Figg*?"

The last unknown was, without question, the most unsettling. Travis had thought that there would never be a level of apprehension greater than the few second before he pulled the trigger on an assassination. He was wrong. His finger trembled as he tried to press the "talk" button.

"Hello," his voice wavered.

"Is Carlos there?"

"Who?" Travis said.

"Carlos."

It was a male voice, thick with a Latino accent. Every muscle in his body released the tension at once. He exhaled two lungs-full of air.

"I think you have the wrong number," he spoke into the mouthpiece.

"Are you sure,… Travis?"

The voice changed. It wasn't a wrong number. His stomach leapt into his throat and he felt like he was going to vomit.

"Do have any idea how badly you've fucked up, Travis?"

Travis couldn't formulate any words. His mouth was as arid as the Sahara.

"I guess you're surprised to hear from me, huh?"

There was more silence.

"Travis? Are you there? Cat got your tongue?"

"What do you want, Figg?"

Travis' tried, unsuccessfully, to keep his voice from cracking.

"Um, jeez. What *do* I want? So kind of you to ask, kid. Lemme' think for a second," he paused.

"How about…YOUR FUCKING INTESTINES WRAPPED AROUND YOUR DECAPITATED HEAD, you worthless little maggot."

Figg was fairly specific. Travis didn't know what to say or where to begin.

"Figg, just hold on a minute, just hold on. Lemme' explain."

"Explain *what*?" Travis asked himself.

"Explain *what*?" Figg said it aloud.

"Explain how you hit me over the head with a *fucking clock radio*! Explain how you left me handcuffed to that bed to bleed to death. Or maybe how you stole my car, my gun, my phone and managed to *completely* screw up everything I had worked so hard to plan."

"Listen, Figg, you didn't leave me a whole lotta choices." It was a meager interjection.

"That was the point you stupid son-of-a-bitch! What is it about blackmail you don't understand, Travis? The whole idea is to eliminate any and all choices. I know you're smarter than that!"

Travis kept thinking about what, if anything, had happened to Mike.

"It's almost like you're *trying* to kill your brother. Is that what you want, Travis? That can still be arranged so very easily."

"No!" Travis was emphatic.

He was relieved that Mike was still alive.

"Well, lucky for you, I've had a little time, and I've been able to put together a contingency plan," Figg said.

"Alright, Alright, tell me what you want me to do."

"Get your ass down to Parkland Emergency, right now. And I swear on everything that is holy, if you try any more heroics, I'll kill you and your retard brother and just take care of this thing myself."

"I'm on my way. Gimme' fifteen minutes."

"You've got ten," Figg replied.

Travis' ray of hope had been suddenly been all but snuffed out. It felt more like it had been burnt out completely. He was absolutely demoralized. Dejected, he took the file of pictures that lay on the floor board and returned them to the trunk. He returned it, along with the AR-15, to exactly where he originally found them. He thought there was a fifty-fifty chance that Figg wouldn't assume that he had gone through the materials. Time appeared to be running out as he navigated through traffic to return the car, as well as any leverage he had fought to attain, back to the demon spawn.

Chapter Twenty Two

PARKLAND MEMORIAL HOSPITAL WAS ONLY a few minutes away down on Harry Hines Boulevard. As he maneuvered through the full weight of rush hour traffic, the nausea was replaced by the ache in the pit of Travis' stomach. It was the ache of helplessness and fear. He wondered how Figg had freed himself and made it to the hospital after having lost so much blood. As he made the turn to Parkland's emergency drop off lanes, he saw Figg just inside the wide, automatic sliding doors. His head was wrapped with several layers of thick gauze bandages. Figg spotted Travis approaching and flicked the butt of his cigarette. It caromed off the back of a hospital employee that was pushing a patient in a wheelchair nearby. The heavy-set male orderly turned around. Figg gave him a look that said:

"What the hell are you gonna' do about it?"

He held both arms out provoking the orderly. The scrub-laden grunt glared at Figg for a few seconds bolstering his manhood, but would never have engaged him. Figg continued about his business as if nothing had happened. It was 7:42 in the a.m. He made a motion to Travis to roll down the window.

"Get out of the car."

He did as he was told. Figg grabbed him under each arm from behind and shoved him to the back end of the car.

"Spread 'em out, let's go."

Figg frisked him from the ankles up.

"Everything is in the front seat." Travis said, referring to the .40 SW, the keys and the cell phone.

He grabbed Travis by the collar of his mangy flannel and bullied him to the front seat.

"Get in."

A trio of other-worlders watched what was going on between the two with curiosity and noticeable disdain.

"What are you fuckheads lookin' at?" Figg asked.

The three turned their heads and proceeded on their way.

They pulled away from the hospital. There was nary a sound in the car for several minutes. Travis never thought he would actually prefer Figg to talk, but his silence proved to be exponentially more nerve racking. If he could've thought of something pertinent to say, he would've. Anything he might say would most certainly be viewed as further insubordination, and would just bring about some form of abuse. The silence was too much. Travis decided to roll the dice.

"Well, aren't you gonna' handcuff me?"

"Do you have a pair of handcuffs?" Figg fired back.

"I know you're not stupid enough to try anything else. There are no more free passes. This is it."

"What about the call-ins with the vice-presidents every hour?" Travis asked.

"Not necessary, they were more for fun than anything else."

Figg smiled.

"I mean, seeing you on the floor of that motel room, about to pass out with fear was priceless. Don't you think? Besides, if I wanted to kill Mike, I could've had it done at any time. Surely you knew that."

Travis was pissed off and embarrassed.

"Is this whole thing just a game to you? Is my pain and suffering no more than a source of amusement to you for God's sake?"

"Does it seem like a game to you, Travis?"

"No, not at all. It seems very much like a nightmare."

"Well, damn, here I am thinking that everybody's having a good time and I find out that my little snitch here is being a wet blanket. What a shame. I guess, for me, it's been pretty much a game, yeah. C'mon, Travis, you gotta' admit, you've had an exciting couple a' days, haven't you?"

The man was not human. Where was the emotion? Travis actually found himself contemplating whether or not he was some sort of lab creation, or maybe a cyborg of some kind. The thought no longer seemed so ridiculous. He wondered if there was even a point in conversing with Figg at all. Some of the things he said made him think that he had lost his grip on reality altogether. But what else could he do? This was the man holding all the cards, sociopathic lunatic or not.

"You really had me fooled, Travis. I thought you were much too smart to do what you did at the motel. How could you leave me there to die? What have I ever done to you?"

Figg truly believed that he had been treated unjustly. His psychoses had blinded him to his own brutality. Travis was quick to remind him.

"You mean other than kidnapping me and Mike, holding him hostage, and forcing me to commit murder? All the while knowing you're going to kill us both when this is over."

Figg grinned wide again.

"Yeah, I mean besides that."

"Do you have even the slightest inkling as to how incredibly mentally ill you are, Figg?"

"Mentally ill, me? Have you seen this big white bandage around my head? You did this. You tried to kill me. I wouldn't say you're the model of sanity yourself."

"I wasn't trying to kill you. I was trying to give me and my brother a chance." Travis wanted to tell Figg just how close he had come to dying in that motel room, but realized that it would only hurt his position further. Instead, Travis justified the assault, as if he needed to.

"So there I am." Figg said. "I wake up and I'm blind in one eye. I'm wondering what the hell just happened. I'm handcuffed to the bedpost. I have no idea what time it is or even what day. After a few minutes of disorientation, I remember the snubbed nose .38 special in my ankle holster. I blow the cuffs off and try to stand up. But you know what, Travis? It was so strange because I couldn't manage to stay on my feet."

Travis sensed the beginning of spectacular bi-polar mood swing.

"I *couldn't stand up*, Travis!" Figg' voice grew louder, then softer as he made another jagged segue.

"I have to say I'm kind of impressed that you were able to fool my friend with that list of Vice Presidents." Figg was getting a welt on his back from patting himself on it. Travis, meanwhile, was fed up with all of his ego stroking and finally decided to let the fire roll off his tongue.

"Oh, man, Figg, you're right, I have no idea how a blue collar grunt like yourself would even know that the office of Vice President existed. And then to be able to memorize so many names in sequence is just flat-out jaw-dropping. I gotta' tell ya', you've got it backwards, pal, *you* amaze *me*. I'm curious, have the rocket scientists at NASA returned your phone calls yet, because if they haven't, it's their loss, believe me. You are in the wrong line of work, man. You should be doing something so much more important than bullying and blackmailing the citizens of this town."

Travis didn't just 'cross the line' with the sarcastic tangent, he flew by it at mach 1. He pretended not to be in complete emotional and physical anticipation of how Figg would react.

Figg's reaction was atypical.

"I was always interested in the Vice Presidents, even as a kid. I don't know why. Everybody thought it was a little strange. Most people could care less about 'em, but I always thought it would be really cool to be one. Did you know that they get travel around the world, live in a *huge*, fuckin' mansion that's probably bigger than the White House and they get paid like $300,000 or somethin' like that for doin' nothin', people waiting hand and foot on them. And to top it all off, you not only get to be the tiebreaker in the Senate, but you have the inside track to becoming the current president's successor. You have to admit, Travis, that's one helluva job.

Figg's lack of brutality in his response wasn't what Travis was expecting. He was calm and spoke softly. Travis knew better than to let his guard down, and was prepared for the inevitable explosion. But, for the next few minutes, none came. After about five minutes, Travis found himself unable to keep such heightened awareness and psychologically began to relax ever so slightly, and he began to think about Figg's strange obsession with Vice Presidents. Without warning and quick as lightning, Figg grabbed the back of Travis' head and smashed it into the dashboard. The pain wasn't dissimilar to the driver's pistol whip two days earlier, perhaps a bit more severe. He brought both hands to his forehead and moaned as the nerve endings reacted to the trauma. When he pulled his hands back, they were red with blood. His face had broken open. He reapplied his hands as blood rushed over his fingers like a babbling brook. He had to apply additional pressure with his shirt.

"You *son of a ...*" he couldn't even finish slandering Figg the pain was so severe.

"What you're feeling right now Travis, isn't one tenth of what I felt. Listen to ya'. You'd think I had just tried to knock your head off."

A few seconds passed.

"Are ya' okay, kid? Good, because I want you to know the rest of what happened after you left. Where was I? Oh yeah. I actually crawled, *crawled,* to the mirror. It wasn't very pretty, Travis. My hair was soaked with blood and the entire left side of my face and neck was covered in blood, too, and part of it had sealed my left eye shut. I think it was at that point when I decided that once this thing is done, you're gonna' feel pain greater than you ever have before. And as for your retard brother, well, you don't want to know the torture he's gonna' experience. I was honestly prepared to spare you both and put you both back on a bus to another city, but now, I just don't think that's gonna' be possible. At least in your case."

Travis got a lump in his throat the size of a lemon. He was too shaken to be angry. Figg issued the threat so matter-of–factly, it couldn't have been laced with any more horror.

"Don't you think that's reasonable, Travis? It's the fairest solution I could come up with. Tell me if you can think of something fairer."

Travis already knew that Figg would kill them both, regardless, but to hear him verbalize it was more bone-chilling than he could ever imagine.

"I understand why you would go ahead and do me, but why would you hurt Mike? He doesn't understand what's happening. He would never be a threat to you, ever."

Travis was fighting an uphill battle as he tried to reason with Figg. His words were muffled as he cupped his blood covered hands over his face and mouth.

"That's simple." Figg said.

"Just having you know the pain he will endure as a result of your actions is all the satisfaction I really need."

Travis face was still pulsating and his eyes were filled with water. He put his head between his knees. All that he could think of was, "here we go again." These thoughts were all too brief, however. When he raised his head, his eyes filled with salty water, he saw what looked like a business card sitting perfectly exposed on the passenger side of the gear box. His vision was blurry from the tears, but he knew what it was. He could make out that it was right side up. All of the fat man's information was showing, including his cell phone number. It had fallen from the chest pocket of his T-shirt when his face was planted into the dash. He looked at Figg out of the corner of his eye while he still applied his shirt to his face. Figg hadn't noticed the card yet.

"You know, I think when you cracked my head open with that clock, it might have affected my thinking a little bit. Are you sensing that my thinking is a little off?"

Travis shook his head.

"You mean *more* than before?"

It was an obvious retort. He slowly moved his left hand from his face to his side. He wanted to keep Figg engaged in conversation and direct his attention away from the card.

"Where are we going?" Travis asked.

Figg offered no answer. They were heading east on I-30. The day was already old to Travis even though it was only eight o'clock in the morning.

He moved his hand from his side and rested his fingers on the console, just shy of the gear box. He was contemplating a quick move for the evidence, but, with his vision and his depth perception at less than one hundred percent, he lacked the gumption. His hand was six inches from the card.

"But, no lists this time. You step outta' line one inch and I'll just make the call. I'm tired of your bullshit, kid. It's so much easier this way."

Travis continued to manipulate his fingers in a pathetic, wounded spider-like fashion. He placed his index finger on the card. He took a final look at Figg out of the corner of his eye. He appeared to be intent on the road ahead. Travis placed his hand over the card. Just as he began to retract his appendage, Figg's hand latched onto his wrist with the voracity of a hungry boa constrictor.

"Would you mind dropping that? *See*, this is exactly what I'm talking about. *Unbelievable*! You are one sneaky, stupid son of a bitch, you know that!"

Travis rolled his eyes, conceding failure. He dropped the card back onto the gear box.

"What do we have here?"

Figg perused the mark's business card.

"Hmmm, I think I know this guy. I didn't know that you did too, Travis. You really should've told me that the two of you had met. I guess my first question is who contacted who? Don't lie to me, kid. I've had just about enough of your lies. So tell me, did he contact you?"

Travis quickly mulled the pros and cons of telling Figg the truth or, misleading him further. If he revealed that the fat man had somehow contacted him, he would come across as having some control over the situation. He would appear to be merely a pawn in whatever the mark had planned for Figg, and he would still have the advantage of plausible deniability.

The alternative would be to admit the truth, and that would push Figg over the edge. He would likely make good on his threat to dispose of him and Mike and go it alone. And he really didn't want to have anything beaten out of him. He already had bruised ribs, broken ring and pinky fingers, a mild concussion and a recently broken nose. Hence, he was going to have to be convincing with his story. Travis still wanted Figg to consider him as little more than a trigger man.

"He contacted me. I don't know how, but somehow he knew who I was. I think it may have been a homeless man in his twenties driving a new unmarked police cruiser. He pulled me over on Commerce Avenue early this morning. That's the truth, I swear to it."

Travis hoped his tale was tall enough.

"You're telling me he just pulled you over. He pulled you over because he thought you looked suspicious. You expect me to believe that?" Figg didn't seem to be buying it. He needed to be more persuasive.

"That's what happened," he said confidently.

"What time did this happen?" Figg tried to nail him down.

"Around seven."

"Seven? Seven o'clock ya' say."

"That's right." Travis maintained.

"I.A. cops don't even get out of bed until eight. *I can't believe you're trying to bullshit me again*!" Figg pounded the steering wheel.

"Hey, I'm not trying to bullshit you, Figg. He knew something else. He wasn't doing some routine traffic bust. He was working a tip or something."

Travis could see that this lie had tempered Figg' cynicism somewhat.

"Well, what did he know? Let's talk about what you two discussed. How 'bout that."

Travis was really working on the fly now. He was getting awfully creative.

"He had picked up some information that you had been seen with me up at the station yesterday. Then he saw the two of us driving away from the precinct together. I mean, c'mon, Figg, it doesn't take an atom-splitter to figure out I'm your snitch. And then he sees me driving around in your car. That was it." Not bad, Travis thought.

"What did you tell him?" Figg asked.

"I told him I was working a drug case. And that I was digging around for you. He did think it was odd that I was driving your car."

Figg had a look on his face like he wasn't sure what to believe.

"Why, is he interested in you?" Travis did his best to sound ignorant.

"Shut up." Figg replied.

"Did he say anything about me, or, anything about an investigation?"

"He mentioned that I might want to steer clear of you for the next twenty-four hours or so. Then he gave me his card and told me to call him if I could provide any further information. That's it. He let me go after that. What does he want? Is he the mark?"

Figg had nothing in the way of a response. He was too busy sorting out the smorgasbord of hogwash Travis had just fed him trying to extract and ascertain any truth from it.

"Alright, we're gonna' have to move this whole thing up even further than I thought." Figg had bought enough of Travis' fictional account to change the plan.

"Move what up?" Travis thought he might be going overboard feigning ignorance. He needed to tone it down.

"The hit's gonna' go down at noon now." Figg said firmly.

"Noon? That's three and a half hours from now."

Travis had been so busy making up a story that he almost forgot he had told the fat man to fly the coop for the rest of the day. He was going to have to get the fat man back in the fray, and fast. He had to get him back to the building on Harwood in less than three hours.

"He is the mark, isn't he?" Travis had to play out the story in order to get to the pertinent parts.

"Yeah. That's the son of a bitch. He's the one you're gonna' take care of. I was gonna' show you his ugly, fat-ass last night, until you decided you'd try and derail your objective." He looked at the business card again.

"Is this his cell phone number he wrote here?" he asked.

"Yeah, it is." Travis got a little bit excited.

He could sense Figg was vulnerable and could now be led down an alternate path. One that Travis might have a little more control over. Still, he had to be careful not to lead him down the wrong path. The major sticking point now concerned how he was going to contact the mark and make him privy to the new agenda.

Chapter Twenty Three

FIGG PULLED OFF THE INTERSTATE and rolled into one of the many parking lots of the Fair Park complex. Fair Park was an enormous collection of buildings just a mile or two southeast of the Beast. The complex included the Music Hall and the Hall of State amongst others. It also boasted the Cotton Bowl and was the perennial home of the State Fair of Texas. He stopped in the middle of a large, empty parking lot and got out of the car. Travis watched Figg move to the front of the vehicle. He appeared to be nervous. He paced back and forth with his hands on his hips. It looked like he was engaged in serious thought. He had been thrown a curveball and didn't seem to be adjusting very well. After about five minutes of wear and tear to the soles of his shoes, he pulled out the cell phone.

Obviously, Travis was very interested in what he had to say. Figg had turned the car off, so Travis didn't have the option of cracking the electric window. Instead, he opened the door just a smidge and did his best to eavesdrop.

"It's time to get the girl," Figg spoke into the phone.

Travis assumed he was talking to his accomplice, the driver.

"I don't care how you do it. Use your badge. Tell 'em her grandmother just croaked. Do whatever you have to. Just get her and take her back, right now!"

Figg paused to listen again.

"Well, there's been a little change. Do you think you can handle that?"

He was visibly irritated by the driver's next question.

"*I don't care*! Take him with you, leave him there. Can't you make one *damn* decision for yourself? Just shut up and listen. She's a second-grader at Dan D. Rogers Elementary on Abrams and Lovers Lane."

Figg had done some extensive research into the mark's background. Travis wasn't surprised. The psychopath paused once more.

"Fine."

He finished his conversation and returned to car. Travis couldn't let Figg know he had overheard the exchange. He waited until Figg got back into the front seat, and as he moved to shut the door, Travis readied to close his simultaneously. He did so successfully.

"What are we doing?" Travis asked.

"*Will you just shut up*? Don't worry about it. This is the absolute last time I'm gonna' say this. You just worry about your objective. You shouldn't be concerned with anything else. *Nothing*!"

Figg was struggling to keep himself together. Whether it was the strain of his current predicament, or, the fact that he was certifiably deranged, he was starting to come apart at the seams. He took a deep breath and exhaled for what seemed like a full minute.

"I want you to call the mark," he said calmly.

"Right now?"

"No, tomorrow. Of course, right now."

"I want you to tell him that you need to meet with him. Tell him you'll come to the office a little before noon," Figg plotted.

"What am I gonna' tell him I need to meet about?" Travis asked.

"Tell him you've got something on me and you need to see him in person."

"What if he wants to get together somewhere else?"

"You tell him that if he wants the information, that you'll bring it to him at a designated location. Otherwise, he won't get anything. Trust me, that fat fuckin' bastard will go after any carrot you dangle in front of him."

He handed Travis the phone. Travis was a little taken aback.

"You want me to call him right now?"

"Sure, why not? Is there some reason you can't call him now?"

"No."

He took the phone. Figg handed him the card with the mark's personal line scribbled on it. Unexpectedly, Travis became terribly nervous. He realized that his choice of words with the mark would be tantamount to keeping Figg in the dark as to their actual rapport with one another. He decided he would keep his statements terse and ambiguous. It would be up to the fat man to play along and follow his lead.

"Yeah, it's Travis, from this morning."

"Yeah, I remember. What is it?" the mark answered.

"I have something on Figg that you'll be very interested to see."

"Okay."

"I'll meet you at your office at, say, eleven forty-five." Travis glanced over at Figg and received a nod of approval.

"What? Wait a minute. You said to stay away from the office. Why do you want to meet there? What's happened? What's going on?"

"If you want it, I need to see you in person. And I need to meet at your office."

Travis looked over at Figg a second time. He was watching and listening intently. The fat man responded.

"Figg's gotten to you hasn't he?"

Travis realized that he could insert a very short answer to the mark's question without arising suspicion.

"Yes, that's right," he said.

The fat man wanted to know more, but didn't know that Travis wasn't in a position to expound.

"What's he planning? You've gotta' tell me what's goin' on if I'm gonna' be able to help."

Travis had to conclude the conversation.

"That's right. Eleven forty-five, at your office on Harwood. Just be there, *please*!"

He pressed the "end" button on the cell phone. He hoped that fat man took note of the emphasis he placed on the word "please". It was the only way he could hint as to the importance of his cooperation, but that he wasn't going to be in any danger by showing up.

"He'll be thcrc," he said to Figg.

"He better be," Figg shot back.

Figg laid some ten or twelve feet of thick tread on the pavement as he pulled a hard u-turn and returned to the Interstate.

"Now that things have changed a little bit, I think you and I should have a quick dress rehearsal and see if we need to make any other adjustments. What da' ya' think?"

Obviously, Figg didn't care what Travis thought, so he didn't bother responding to the rhetoric. He was more concerned with how, and if, he would be able to establish clear communication with the mark. Until he did, he was in a position of having to hope that the fat man would walk right into the fire and trust someone he had no reason to. Whatever he was going to do, he had to do it quickly. The clock read 9:48.

Chapter Twenty Four

There's something romantic about the notion of two men entering an arena, and only one man leaving. Whether it be a gunfight, a boxing match, or an assassination.

IT WAS A CLEAR MORNING AND the golden glare of the rising sun was everywhere. They were heading west, back to the target zone. Travis was still trying to stop the bleeding from the bridge of his nose, compliments of his demented companion. He pinched his nose with his thumb and index finger. He could feel the bone and cartilage jiggling in his grip.

"I hope you're happy. You broke my nose, you prick!"

"Now that's just plain sad," Figg said.

"A marine complaining about a little thing like a broken nose. If you're the example of what the Corps is turning out nowadays, this country is in a world a' shit."

Travis was getting tired of Figg' insults.

"You wouldn't last two days in boot camp." He lobbed a rare insult back at Figg.

Figg smiled.

"You don't think so, huh?"

"That's right, forty-eight hours and you'd be crying like a baby."

"You mean like you're crying right now over your poor little nose?" Figg' barb was below the belt and actually stung just a little. Travis changed the subject.

"Why do we have to go over this again? The only thing that's changed is the time. I need somethin' to eat. I haven't eaten in a day. I'm gettin' lightheaded over here."

"Oh, c'mon, you are such high maintenance. Ya' know that? You remind me of my second ex-wife." Figg was exasperated.

Travis reinforced his position.

"I'm serious. I need some food," he said.

"Fine, we'll pick somethin' up somewhere for poor, little Travis."

There was silence in the car for the next ten or fifteen minutes as they entered the Beast for the last time. One of them wouldn't leave the city's core alive. There was a strange, quiet tenseness between them.

Travis decided he would broach the most delicate of subjects.

"Why should I do this?" He asked.

"What do you mean, '*Why should I do this?* '"

"Well, let's be honest, if you're gonna' kill me and Mike regardless, how does it benefit me to do this?"

"What makes you think I won't let you live? Have I ever said that you wouldn't walk away from this? Have you ever thought about the possibility of me sticking you guys on a bus outta' town with the understanding that I'll never see you in Dallas again?"

Travis was understandably cynical.

"You expect me buy that with all that talk earlier about the pain. The kinda' pain I've never felt before and how just knowing the pain Mike's gonna' feel. What about all of that?"

"Oh, *that*?" Figg said.

"I was really pissed off when I said that. Sometimes I say things I don't mean when I'm upset. I'm sure you can understand that, kid. I don't believe I've ever said a word about killing either one of you. Correct me if I'm wrong."

"You really think I'm an idiot, don't you?" he asked.

"Of course not, Travis."

"You expect me to believe that you're gonna' let me, the assassin for your premeditated murder of a Dallas Internal Affairs officer, walk away? I don't care if you say I can take a trip to China, it's all about eliminating any links. I know that and so do you."

Figg pursed his lips considering Travis' remarks.

"Well, maybe you're right. How 'bout if I said that Mike will definitely live. Certainly you'd want that to happen, wouldn't you?"

"What do you think?" Travis obliged.

"I think you'd do anything if there was even a 5 percent chance that Mike would survive. You probably think that's noble don't you? You think that makes you some kinda martyr. I think it's the one thing that makes you weak. It makes you vulnerable. Love is an ugly thing. It prevents men from realizing their full potential."

Travis desperately tried to identify with what Figg was saying. He tried to understand, on the most basic level, the ideology of someone bereft of goodness. It was impossible.

"Their full potential as *what*?" He asked.

"As the impervious masters of their society. As the lions of the jungle, as the Great White in the deep blue sea. See, Travis, I operate at the very top of the food chain. And I'm able to do that because I don't allow myself to be burdened with petty emotions like love."

Travis listened, unable to respond to what he had just heard. Figg had allowed him another quick peek into his warped, rusted out mind and it left him speechless.

They pulled into a gas station just outside the Beast. Travis still held his shirt to his face.

"Let's go to the bathroom and clean your face up. We can't have you walking around looking like that."

Figg walked around the car and stood a few paces behind Travis. He pushed Travis toward the rear of the car and popped the trunk.

"Get the jumpsuit."

The two walked to the bathroom that was off on the side of the station. Figg checked the bathroom to make sure there weren't any escape routes. It was more out of habit than anything else. Satisfied, he motioned Travis inward.

"Clean yourself up."

He gave Travis a slight shove as he walked by, again, out of habit.

"Are you gonna' close the door or just stand there?" Travis wanted a moment to himself.

"No, I think I'll stand right here. Fool me once shame on you, well, you know the rest."

Travis looked at his severely swollen nose in the cracked mirror. It was almost twice its normal size and had taken on a yellowish-green hue. Blood had run down over his lips, down his chin and neck. He proceeded to gingerly apply water to the bloodied areas.

"Hurry up!"

Figg pressured him.

"Hold on! You're the reason I'm having to do this. You fucking douche bag." The last half he muttered under his breath.

Figg checked his watch.

"We've got two hours and I want to go over a few things," he demanded.

Travis stepped into the jumpsuit, pulled it over his shoulders and zipped it all the way up.

"You can put the rest on later." Figg said.

"Fine."

"What about some food?" Travis asked.

"God, will you quit your bitchin'? Let's go in there and get poor, little Travis somethin' to eat."

As Travis made his way to the convenience store inside the station, Figg continued to shadow him. There were no other customers. They walked up and down the food aisle. Travis grabbed some powdered donuts and a big bag of potato chips. He went to the refrigerated doors and selected a half-gallon of milk.

"Are you sure that's enough milk?" Figg had to say *something.*

"That's enough. C'mon, let's go up front."

Travis laid the items on the counter. The clerk was sitting behind the counter, reading a piece of tabloid trash. The headline read, "*Woman Gives Birth to Cloned Rabbit*".

"Hey, you wanna' ring us up here?" Figg said.

"I'm comin'." The clerk replied as if he had been put out.

The pony-tailed man looked Travis up and down. His black jumpsuit and busted nose were reason enough to be a little suspicious, not to mention Figg' mummified, gauze-wrapped head. Neither had shaved in the better part of a week. They were a motley pair.

"Is that all?" he asked.

"Yeah." Figg answered.

He began to ring the items on the register.

"Wait a second."

Figg stuck his hand into a jar full of beef jerky and tossed a fistful of the dried meat pieces onto the counter.

"Gimme' a pack of those, on the end there."

He pointed to a particular brand of cigarettes.

"Oh, what the hell. I'll take a six pack a' beer while I'm at it," he said.

"I'm sorry, pal. I can't sell you alcohol until after twelve on Sundays. It's state law. I've got the chains on the doors back there." The clerk pointed to the beer portion of the refrigerator.

"I'm sorry, could you repeat that?" Figg said.

Travis could feel something awful was about to happen to the clerk. Figg squinted his eyes and leaned forward to read the man's nametag.

"Listen, Richard, do you mind if I call you *Dick*? I don't give a shit about any state law. Are you gonna' sell me some beer or not?"

Unfortunately, the clerk thought he was dealing with the typical, surly customer.

"No, I'm not. And if you have a problem with that, then maybe I can call the cops and they can help us figure this out."

Travis rolled his eyes and dropped his head. The clerk had poked the gorilla with a stick one too many times, and the result was going to be ugly. Figg smiled.

"Oh, no! Please don't do that? I don't want to get the authorities involved," he said with a wry smile.

"Alright then." The clerk began to total the items on the cash register.

Figg's gun appeared as if out of nowhere. He pressed the barrel square on the clerk's forehead.

"Put your hand on the counter," Figg demanded.

Travis could smell the odor of ammonia consistent with urine and noticed a dark stain start to spread down Richard's right pant leg.

"Hey, look at this. Look, Travis. Dick here pissed his pants. You know, Dick, you are one pathetic little bastard," Figg was almost giddy.

"Listen, just wait a second." Richard's voice cracked and quivered.

"Just let me unlock the doors and you can have whatever you want, okay."

Figg shook his head.

"You already had a chance to do that. Now put you're hand on the counter right now!"

He placed his hand face up on the wood counter top. As if bracing for intense pain, the helpless clerk closed his eyes.

"Open your eyes," Figg said sternly.

The clerk didn't comply.

"I said, *open your damn eyes*!"

He slowly did as he was told. Figg looked directly at Travis, who was standing to the right of him, away from the door. He had the same crazed look in his eyes that he had on the street a few nights earlier when he was holding his gun to Mike's head after they had been taken off the bus.

"I want you to see this," he said.

"See what. Why are you doing this?" Travis asked, dumbfounded.

"I want you to understand what I mean by existing at the top of the food chain."

Travis looked at the clerk. He was looking right back at him. He had a look on his face that pleaded, "Please do something." But there wasn't anything he could do. And at that moment, Figg lifted his jacket above his belt on his left side and unsnapped a sleeve that held a six inch knife. In one quick, sweeping motion he pulled it from its cover and hurled the steel blade in a downward motion, planting it in the middle of the clerk's palm cutting his 'life-line' in half pinning his hand to the counter like a tack through paper on a bulletin board. Travis turned his head away as the clerk's shriek reverberated throughout the store. Figg guided Travis to the rear of the store where the refrigerated items were located. He stepped forward and proceeded to fire a round shattering the glass door that insulated all of the alcohol.

"Travis, come here."

He complied.

"Grab me a six pack."

Travis stepped lightly on the broken glass. It crackled under his feet. He pulled the beer from the rack.

"There's just one more thing we have to do." Figg said.

Travis, still hungry, remembered to get the food on the counter. The clerk still had his hand stapled to the counter top. He moaned as he held his forearm with his other hand. They both watched, helpless, as an amoeba-shaped pool of blood oozed across the surface and spilled off the edge like a scarlet waterfall. Figg walked up right behind Travis and approached the clerk again.

"One more thing, Dick, if you could just tell me where the security tapes are you'd really save me and my friend here a whole lotta' time," he spoke calmly putting the gun back to his forehead.

The clerk was closing in on a complete state of shock from the loss of blood and was more or less incoherent. His eyes were like slits and he didn't respond.

"C'mon Figg, he's losing consciousness, he can't even answer you," Travis chimed in.

"Useless fuck." Figg pulled his gun back and the clerk's head fell to the counter with a loud thump.

"I'm gonna' have to do this myself," he said as he holstered his weapon.

Figg had a couple of department buddies in robbery homicide who had imparted upon him the whereabouts of most convenience store security camera's, especially at smaller "mom 'n pop" establishments like this one. The knife was the only thing holding the clerk upright. Figg leaned all the way over the counter trying to avoid the pint of plasma that blanketed the area and ripped the medium-sized metal ring holding a half-a-dozen or so keys from the clerk's belt. With Travis by his side, he walked to the rear of store and stopped in front of the white door that read 'employees only'. He began trying keys. The third key slid cleanly in and turned. Inside were shelves filled to the ceiling with excess inventory and supplies including paper cups, lids, paper towels and such. Figg began clearing out the shelves and instructed Travis do the same.

"What type of recording device are we looking for exactly?" Travis asked, somewhat naively.

"You'll know when you see it."

Figg climbed the shelves to reach higher, and again, instructed Travis to do likewise.

"There you are." Figg exclaimed as he swept boxes of drinking straws aside to reveal a large metal box with fastened with a padlock. He hopped back down to the floor and stacked plastic crates at the foot of the shelf containing the box. Once atop the makeshift ladder, he leveraged himself a little and wrapped his arms around the box. With one quick, forceful tug, he freed the box from the wiring in the rear and cradled it in his arms.

"Here." He handed the box to a grounded Travis and jumped leeward.

"Put it on the ground," Figg demanded as he cleared an area away with his foot.

Without hesitation, Figg proceeded to draw his gun, plant his right foot squarely on top of the box, aim at the padlock, and look away as he fired a single round piercing the padlock's core and rendering it useless. Inside were two VCR's.

"Here, carry these," Figg handed the VCR's to Travis and guided him out and back to the front of the store.

Figg abruptly yanked the knife from the clerk's hand, and he collapsed to the floor.

"Next time, I suggest you just get me the beer." He was smug.

Travis was disturbed at the sight of someone's blood other than his own, but he was famished to the point that he picked the blood soaked food items from the counter and balanced them atop the VCR's he was carrying. As they approached the door to leave, a car pulled up next to the gas tank to fill up. The middle-aged man inside opened his door and caught a glimpse of Travis toting two VCR's, and Figg, simply looking like Figg. He closed his car door, hastily started the car and sped away.

The bells on the door jingled as Figg was kind enough to hold the door for his unwilling accomplice.

"I guess he didn't like the price per gallon." Figg issued another bad joke, referring to the man fleeing the scene.

As the pair got almost all the way to the car, Figg stopped in his tracks.

"Hold on a second. I forgot my beef jerky."

Chapter Twenty Five

FIGG TORE A BEER FROM ITS plastic ring, popped the top and slammed it. He ripped away at the beef jerky like a hyena tearing away at the last scraps of an animal carcass. The plastic wrapping had Dick's blood dripping from it. He took a second beer and abused it the same way he did the first. A bellowing belch ensued that would've sent small animals scurrying for the hills. It appeared to Travis like Figg was trying to relieve some stress through self-medication.

"Ya' know my dad used to be able to slam twelve of these every night before he passed out. I could probably do six or seven, but we have some rather important business to take care of here in an hour or so. Don't wanna' be impaired." He looked at Travis and winked.

"When we get there, I'm going to leave the car down in the parking garage of the building. I'm gonna' leave you in the car, *alone*, and deliver the goods upstairs to room 505."

"How are you gonna' carry a rifle up to the fifth floor without being seen?" Travis interrupted.

"*Don't worry about that.* I am *so* glad this thing is almost over. I don't think I can stomach being around you much more. All you need to remember is that if you're anywhere other than exactly where I tell you to be, I *will not* hesitate to have Mike killed. Are we one-hundred percent clear on that?"

"Yes, we are."

Travis was rudely reminded of his subservience.

"Alright then, good."

They were just a block away now as the time was nearing eleven A.M. They pulled into the garage parking ramp of the building. Figg parked the car close to the east-side stairwell door. He got out and popped the trunk. He took the rifle case, the flak jacket, gloves and hat and slammed the trunk shut. He tossed everything but the rifle across the driver's seat into Travis' lap.

"Put it on," he ordered.

And with that, he disappeared with the rifle behind the stairwell door.

Travis fumbled around with the items as he began to get into the jacket. It was eleven fifteen and he could feel the nervous tension in the pit of his stomach. As he slipped his fingers into the black leathery gloves, he noticed his hands trembling ever so slightly. This was not a good sign. He thought to himself,

"If I'm already shaking right now, what will it be like when I have to pull the trigger?"

He pulled the bill of the cap firmly down over his forehead just above his eyebrows. It was an unbelievably surreal feeling. Here he sat, in the front seat of a 'police officer's' car, dressed in black from head to toe, wearing a bulletproof vest. He was less than forty-five minutes away from a life-altering, and perhaps a life-ending, experience. Travis found himself going over the last few years of his life that had landed him in his current situation. There were so many things he wished he could change, namely, ever getting involved with the man who was, at present, planting the weapon he was to use to kill an innocent police officer. But nothing he had done wrong before this point really mattered now. All that did matter was what he did from this moment forward. Figg reappeared and got back behind the wheel. He was quiet. Travis noticed that Figg seemed a little nervous as well. It was strange to observe Figg experiencing very real, human emotions. He was monitoring the time very carefully.

"It's go time," he said.

The pit in Travis' stomach began to spring butterflies. Figg pulled the phone from his coat pocket and dialed.

"There is a bomb in the building at 832 S. Harwood Street. This is more than a threat. It will detonate within the hour."

There it was. As simple as that, the stage had been set. Travis took the time to remember where Figg returned his phone.

"It's time to play ball, kid. I'm gonna' start heading to the front of the building. Here, take this."

He opened the glove compartment and removed a digital watch. He synchronized it with his.

"When this thing reads twelve o'clock sharp, you make your way to the front and enter the building."

"What if the mark doesn't show?" Travis asked.

This was still a real concern as he was unable to contact him since their phone conversation in the Fair Park parking lot.

"If he doesn't show, well, all hell's gonna' break loose."

Figg started the car and pulled out of the garage. He went north on Harwood and turned right onto the nearest side street on the east side of the block.

"I'll be seeing you in about ten minutes."

Travis sat in the car while Figg got out and turned the corner onto S. Harwood and disappeared from view. Travis put the cheap watch around his wrist and waited. It would be the longest ten minutes of his life. He closed his eyes and took several long, deep breaths. With all the mental willpower he could muster, he tried to organize his thoughts. He tried to summon all the positives while filtering out the negatives. In the back of his mind, unfortunately, there was a certain question he couldn't elude: "How am I going to react when that rifle is in my hands?"

Would he be sent, reeling, into another nightmarish flashback and be unable to focus at all? It was a definite possibility. He knew he would have to block out everything in order to carry out *his* objective. With his adrenaline now whipping his fear into submission and his watch reading high noon, he got out of the car and headed to the front of the building.

Chapter Twenty Six

We cheer for the underdog because most of us drink from the same well he does.

"HELLO," THE FAT MAN PICKED up his office phone.

"I've got your little girl."

"Who is this?" he asked.

"You don't recognize my voice?" Figg answered.

"No."

"Lemme' give you a hint. You killed my son and now you want to put me away for doin' my job. Ring a bell?"

"Please, Lieutenant Figg, don't do anything stupid. I didn't kill your son. It was a gang-related drive-by and you know it. It was bound to happen eventually anyway. Put my daughter on. I wanna' hear her voice."

"She can't talk right know, and, for the record, we both know it wouldn't have happened had you not tried to get him to rat on his old man."

"You sick son of a bitch! I swear..."

Figg cut him off.

"Spare me the 'protective father, if-you-touch-her' bullshit! You never even gave me chance to save my boy, consider yourself lucky she's not already dead. Just do exactly as I tell you, and you might see her again."

"You had eighteen years to save his life, but you never bothered to-" Figg cut off the suddenly brazen mark.

"*Shut the fuck up! Shut the fuck up right now or her head will be in a thousand little pieces! Got it*?"

"Okay, calm down. What do you want me to do?" the fat man shelved his attitude.

"I just want to talk about my case, that's all."

"Where? When?"

"One step at a time, you fat fuck. Gather all the information that you've got on me in the next five minutes, and I mean *everything*, case files, floppy files, photographs. The whole nine yards, got it.

"Yes, I undcrstand," the mark answered.

"Put it in a case and leave it at the east end of your building. Then walk to your car. Don't get in the car. I'll call you with further instructions."

"I can't get all that together in five minutes," the fat man complained.

"There's that much, huh? Well, my suggestion to you would be to get started or you can kiss little Samantha goodbye."

"*No, Oh No! Alright, Alright*! I'll do it!"

Once he heard Figg call his daughter by name, the mark was fully convinced that this was no bluff.

"Glad to hear it."

Figg slid his phone into the front pocket of his leather jacket. He exited the lobby of the building and returned to the fray.

Dressed in his dark jumpsuit, black flak jacket and black cap and gloves, Travis turned the corner onto S. Harwood. There was a crowd of people that had been evacuated from the building. The headcount must've been in the neighborhood of two to three hundred people strewn in front of the building's entrance and stretching across and along the street. Just as he had said, Figg was standing in front of the building entrance, closest to him, as he approached. He had put on a dark baseball cap to conceal the bandages around his head. He was motioning a group of four or five perplexed cubicle clock-watchers away from the door. Figg saw Travis coming closer and began to move with his back at an angle in order to clear a narrow path for Travis to take straight to the door. As he walked around and through Figg's screen, he gently bumped against his exposed front side. Figg turned, accompanying him through the door. He said two words under his breath,

"Seven minutes."

This was how long he had before the actual bomb squad arrived on the scene. He had more like twenty minutes before they would get to his fifth floor perch. For a just a split second before they entered, Travis turned and looked across the street at the mark's car and noticed that Figg's view of the target area was clear and unfettered.

"*Move your ass*, Travis."

He grabbed his arm pulling him through the door. They walked into the lobby unnoticed. He escorted Travis through the lobby without incident. As they reached the elevators Figg took hold of Travis' shoulder. He pulled him close and looked directly into his eyes. They stood, nose to nose.

"I've given you a second opportunity to make the right decision. You just think about Mike, and don't even think about fuckin' with me again, got it?"

The elevators had been shut down as a part of the bomb threat response protocol, so Figg pushed Travis in the direction of the stairwell approximately twenty yards down at the end of the hall. He watched as Travis opened the door and entered the stairwell. Figg waited for the door the close behind him and retreated from inside the building. He looked at his watch. Figg had estimated it would take Travis approximately three minutes to arrive at the window of room #505. It would take another minute for Travis to take his position, ready himself and his weapon. He continued to deal with the confused building inhabitants on the street.

"Move away from the building. There was a bomb threat called in and I need you all to please move across the street until we can verify its legitimacy. Now just move on back, please."

As Figg pushed the people from his line of vision, Travis made haste up a single flight of stairs on east side stairwell, where he was supposed to go up to the fifth floor and take his position in room #505. Instead, he stopped between the first and second floors. He took a long deliberate breathe. His decision had been made, but he needed to organize his thoughts. He paced in small concentric circles at the platform of the staircase, and pulled a cell phone out of the hip pocket of his jumpsuit. It was Figg's. When he was on top of his game, all it took was a gentle brush-by to pick a pocket clean. Figg never felt or suspected a thing. Travis had memorized the mark's number.

"I told you, I'm going to cooperate. Give me a second to get all the materials together."

The mark incorrectly assumed the call was from Figg. Travis didn't have time to delve into the nature of the odd greeting.

"Listen to me if you want to your daughter to live."

"Who is *this*?" The fat man was now thoroughly confused.

"We talked early this morning, remember?"

"Hey, you know Figg has my daughter and is blackmailing me right now? I just got off the phone with him."

"I guess we have a mutual interest now, don't we? So shut up and listen. Maybe we'll both get what we want out of this. When you get to your car, I want you to appear as if you know absolutely nothing about what's goin' on."

"That won't be hard, I *don't* have any idea what's goin' on."

"Look across the street to the entrance of the old, office building with all the commotion out front. You'll be able to see him through the crowd because he wants to make sure he can see you. He'll be hugging the corner of the entrance way closest to you under the green canopy. He'll be trying to conceal himself, so you may only see him peering around. He's wearing a dark baseball cap. This part is very important. *Keep an eye on him*, but don't make it obvious that you are looking at him, just turn your head, keeping him in the periphery of your vision. In about three or four minutes, you'll notice that he will no longer be there. When you don't see him for fifteen seconds or so, I need you to look over to the east side of the building. I'll be standing there waiting for a signal from you to cross the street. Do you understand?"

"Yes, but how will I signal you?"

"Do you smoke?"

"*What*?"

"God Dammit, *do you smoke*?"

"Yes."

"Well, light one up and that'll be my signal. Got it?"

"Yeah, I got it."

You could hear the fear mounting in the fat man's voice. As Travis hung up the phone, he was to room #505.

Figg kept looking at his watch. Three minutes had passed. He retreated behind the corner of the entranceway under the hunter green canopy. He no longer catered to the concerns of the displaced desk jockeys. He fidgeted, looking at his watch every few seconds, anxiously awaiting the culmination of two-and-half days of headaches. Another few seconds passed and he crept to the edge of the entryway. He maneuvered into a spot where he could once again see the target zone clearly.

Inside room 505, Figg had placed the rifle beneath one of the two windows, still in its case and unassembled. The binoculars were next to the AR-15. Travis placed them on the sill closest to the east side of the room so he'd be able to spot the window from the outside, and hopefully, lure Figg to it. He grabbed the case and moved as quickly as he could back to the stairwell. He went all the way down, passed the first floor, back to the underground garage lot. In a full sprint, he made his way up the exit ramp and out of the garage, stopping at the east side corner of the building. As he looked across the street, he saw the mark exit the building with a large satchel. He began to walk away from the lot toward the east end corner of the building.

"Where the hell are you going?" Travis said to himself.

The thought that the mark was going to get Mike and him killed crossed his mind. He disappeared around the corner briefly and reappeared, sans satchel. Travis watched as he walked at an up-tempo pace all the way back across the face of the building and stationed himself by the right rear fender of his car.

Figg muttered softly to himself.

"Right there you big, bald son of a bitch. Stay right there Your head looks like a shiny, ripe watermelon. Kaboom, baby!"

Figg fixated on the rectangular reflection of the sun coming off of the mark's head. He was ready to watch it explode. Any second now…

"You have no idea you're about to take your last breath," Figg was getting off.

"Take the shot, you little maggot. *Where's the shot*?"

Figg was growing more and more concerned with every passing second. The mark had been standing in the target zone for more than two minutes and no shot had been fired. He started clutching his fists and cursing Travis. Another sixty seconds passed. His patience ran out. He entered the building and made a beeline to the east side stairwell.

Out of the corner of his eye, the mark saw that Figg had disappeared for approximately twenty seconds, and, nervously, did as he was told, scrambling for his pack of unfiltered cigarettes and his butane lighter. Travis saw him fumbling and didn't wait for him to light it. He galloped across Harwood, holding the rifle case parallel to his body away from the commotion. He got to the mark's white sedan and sat on the pavement with his back against the front left tire away from the building.

"What's goin' on?" The mark was still in the dark.

Travis looked up and noticed the mark looking down at him.

"*Look up*! Act like I'm not even here. Just tell me when you see Figg in that window with the binoculars on the ledge."

"Okay." The mark was beginning to get a glimpse of what was happening.

Travis frantically began piecing together the weapon. A normal assembly time for the AR-15 is sixty seconds. He took the small flathead screwdriver from the case's side pocket and fastened the scope into place over the barrel stock. He took quickly rotated the eight inch silencer to the barrel's mouth until it was tight. He snapped the sling to the gun and wrapped it twice around his elbow, just as he had back in the corps. There was no time to adjust the specs and he decided against using the bi-pod. He was finished assembling in forty-five seconds. Travis held the rifle in his lap. He exhaled very slowly and closed his eyes. The gravity of what was about to take place came over him like a monsoon. He would have one shot. He placed his hands on the gun. The evil anxiety began to rear its ugly head. He closed his eyes even more firmly and engaged in mental combat with his demons. Travis pounded away at the legion of souls of every mark he had ever killed. He saw their mangled faces and their bloodied, hollowed out cranial cavities. He listened to them. They were all saying the same thing:

"*You didn't even know me... Why?...You didn't even know me.*"

The visions and the voices were so visceral in nature that Travis began to sweat and the muscles in his face became flexed and taut.

"I had no choice. I was just a kid. It was my job." Travis answered them in his head.

The demons continued, in unison,

"*Why?*"

"I'm sorry for what I've done. It was never personal.

I was just following orders. What else do you want me to say? If I could go back and change things, I would. But I can't. Why can't you understand that? Please, you have to let me go."

The battle was intense. It all took place over a span of ten or fifteen seconds. Travis was taking back control over the situation. The legion began to retreat. He advanced, aggressively reclaiming large chunks of his psyche. His resolve was becoming more and more galvanized with every passing second.

It took Figg all of twenty seconds to climb five flights of stairs. He opened the door to the hallway. He drew his weapon, unsure of what he might encounter. Room 505 was no more than ten yards down, on the left. He took long, deliberate strides as he came upon the room. With both hands on his pistol, he put his cheek to the door frame. Three…two…one, he swung around and hurled himself into the room. It was empty with the exception of the pair of binoculars resting on the window sill. He lowered his gun and returned it to its holster.

"That little son of a bitch!" He let his guard down.

This was the last straw. It was time to give the order. Figg reached into his coat pocket for his phone to have Mike and the girl executed. It was the same pocket that always held the phone.

But on this occasion, it was empty. He patted himself up and down hoping to feel something. It was gone.

"I don't believe this," he said aloud.

He gave himself a second, quick frisking. Nothing.

He walked over to the window. He spotted the mark's car still in the same spot. The fat man was also still standing next to it. He dropped down and backed against the wall beneath the window and grabbed the binoculars that he had intended for Travis.

"What do you want me to see, you little maggot?" he asked softly, rhetorically, preparing to peer over the sill.

He turned, raised his head to the window and held the binoculars to his eyes.

The focus of the binoculars was sharp. He scanned the area beneath, finally landing on the mark and his car.

"There he is. He's at the window!" The mark lowered his head and wiped at his nose as he spoke to keep from arousing suspicion.

Travis heard the mark's words in the background amidst his psychological combat. At that moment, all the demons and disfigured images vanished and their voices were quiet. A faint light appeared from distance and gradually came closer. Haloed inside, Travis could make out a man with his back to him sitting outside on a wide, log-splitting stump. He was cleaning the barrels of his .12 gage shotgun. Travis' viewpoint whipped around the man as time sped up ten times normal and he came to an abrupt stop. It was his Dad. He was healthy and strong, dressed in his dark green hunter's vest, a plaid shirt and jeans, just the way Travis always remembered him. Dad blew the powder from the gun's barrels, looked up and smiled.

"It's alright, son, take the shot," he said.

He snapped quickly back to the task at hand brimming with confidence and intense concentration. He began to search the rifle case for ammunition. Two .223 caliber bullets spilled onto the pavement and rolled in opposite directions. He grabbed them, putting one in his pocket, and holding the other in his hand. He pulled back on the bolt, opening the chamber and carefully inserted it. Firmly, he bolted it through. He held the rifle to his chest and rotated to a position on one knee. Next, he placed the weapon on the hood of the mark's car. The scope was blurry. He turned the focus band. The crosshair was dancing wildly on the face of the building. He sharpened the view and began to harness the bull's eye.

"He's holding the binoculars to his eyes." The fat man provided the commentary.

"Quit talking," Travis ordered.

He began to hone in on the target zone. He counted five floors, story by story. He panned right, room by room. He spotted Figg. His heart began to thump wildly.

"He's looking right at us. Do something. *Pull the trigger*!"

The fat man ignored Travis' instruction and began to panic. Travis tuned him out. The shot was there. Figg head was completely exposed. From this distance, there was nothing standing between him and an easy kill. He softly stroked the trigger with his right index finger. He took firm hold of barrel stock. He entered a zone in his mind. It all came back to him, like riding a bike. The feeling brought a little smile to his face, moreover, it carried with it an even stronger sense of confidence. He had one last thing to say to the ebbing legion of inner-demons.

"Make room for one more."

He squeezed the soft trigger.

Final thought for Figg:

"Travis, you sure have got yourself a brass set of-"

The bullet passed through the binocular lenses with an ever so soft "chink", and entered his cranium through his right eye socket. It ripped the brain tissue and the exit wound sent pieces of skull and blood whipping through the air like shrapnel. The trajectory and sheer velocity of the shot lifted him of off his knees and threw him several yards onto his back. He lay there, still, for a few seconds. Then the nerves carried out their final instructions as the demon's right leg flopped like a freshly hooked blue gill on a boat deck. The animal had been put down.

All Travis saw was Figg' head come apart, and him falling from view like a cardboard target at a shooting gallery. He had slain the beast. Travis took a few seconds as he brought the rifle down to his body and he sat against the fender of the car. His immediate thoughts concerned how he had single-handedly made the world a far greater place simply by eliminating one of its most abominable evils. It was truly a case of 'addition by subtraction'.

"Oh my God! You got him. You killed him," the fat man exclaimed.

"You act like you've never seen a man die. You are a cop, aren't you?" Travis was irked by the wide-eyed remark.

"Well, I've never seen anything… like that."

Travis threw the AR-15 in the backseat.

"Lemme' drive," he demanded.

The fat man tossed him the keys and waddled around to the front seat.

Travis turned the keys and gunned the car in reverse out of the parking space. He tried to quickly maneuver the car out of the lot. Several evacuated other-worlders blocked the exit. Travis stuck his head out of the window.

"Get out of the way… *move your ass*!" he yelled.

They moved at a leisurely pace. Travis inched forward, frustrated. He felt like pushing them out of the way with the car's bumper.

"How much time do we have?" the fat man threw his cigarette butt out the window.

"It depends on whether he got the call off to the driver. He would've had to have found another phone."

Travis flung Figg' cell phone out the window. It shattered against the curb.

"If he did, we don't have much. If he didn't, then it depends on how long he'll wait before smelling a rat."

The fat man's anxiety had evolved into an out-and-out panic again.

"What do you think he'll do with my daughter?" he asked, not really wanting to hear the answer.

"He may just leave her. He may take her. I really can't tell you for sure. Either way, though, she'll stay alive until he figures out what's going on. Just pray I can find my brother before he gets a clue."

Travis floored the accelerator and they flew onto Central Expressway. He and the fat man were headed back to search for the warehouse where Mike and the little girl waited.

Chapter Twenty Eight

And the meek shall inherit the earth.

THEY SPED ALONG THE EXPRESSWAY heading south. The Beast was contained on its east side by this particular stretch of road. The skyscrapers towered over there right shoulder as they drove past. Travis took the Interstate 30 merge ramp and curled around and onto it. It went eastbound. Again, he accelerated, asking for the full performance from the V-8 engine. It was around 12:30 p.m., so the traffic was quite a bit lighter than usual.

"What are you planning to do when we get there?"

It was a fair question for the fat man to ask, considering his daughter was involved and they were darting through traffic in his car.

"I have no idea. I'm just trying to decide how I'm gonna' go about finding this place," Travis replied.

"What do you know about its location?"

"I know that it is less than a mile south of the Interstate. It is about three miles east of Deep Ellum." Travis stated confidently.

"*That's it*? That could take hours to find." The fat man was cynical. He continued,

"Did you see anything? Any landmark or distinguishable feature that might help?" he asked.

"No, I told you, we were blindfolded. Everything I know, I heard," Travis shot back, annoyed.

The fat man persevered, unaware that he had engaged in an interrogation type line of questioning.

"You were blindfolded the whole time, even while you were in the warehouse. You couldn't see out a window or anything?"-

"Do me a favor will ya' Mikey?"

"Okay."

"I want you to look out that window up there and tell me what you see."

"Do you see any buildings or road signs or anything like that?"

"Four million clouds."-

Travis looked over at the fat man with a look on his face like he had just discovered gravity, electricity and a cure for cancer, all at that very moment.

"What is it?" the fat man asked.

"*Four million clouds*!" he said. "*Four million clouds*! When he looked outside the window, he saw the four million and clouds"

The fat man was at a loss.

"What the hell does 'four million and clouds' mean?"

He asked another fair question. Travis was sure he had put a piece of the puzzle together.

"Do you play the lottery?" he asked the fat man.

"Sometimes."

"What's the jackpot right now?" Travis asked, impatiently, waiting to hear what he was ninety-five percent sure he already knew.

A smile replaced the look of vexation on the fat man's face and he confirmed:

"It's four million dollars."

They started looking for the Texas lottery billboard alongside the interstate. On the hazy edge of the horizon, a billboard inched closer and closer to the speeding car just south of the highway. As they came close enough to clearly see the jackpot number, Mike's riddle had been solved.

"Mikey, you beautiful, beautiful, boy."

Travis had never been more proud of his big brother in all his life. As they exited just shy of the billboard, on Ferguson Road, Mike instructed the fat man.

"Look for a small, rectangular window on one of the warehouses where you could see that lottery billboard."

Between the two of them, they we're able to narrow it down to two large structures less than a quarter-mile off of the interstate. The warehouses ran lengthwise, parallel to the interstate, and were almost identical. Naturally, they both had the stained windows that Travis remembered from being inside, so they would have a fifty-fifty shot at guessing the right one first. Travis drove slowly as he approached the initial building. He remembered the pitter-patter of the rain that night hitting a tin canopy overhead just before they entered. He parked the car in the rear of the structure. He reached for the rifle in the backseat and got out of the car. The fat man pulled his police issue 9mm. from his belt holster and followed Travis' lead. They walked briskly along the side of the building. Travis needed to know quickly if they had the right one. Bermuda grass and weeds had grown to a knee-high level at its perimeter. The intermittent whizzing of speeding cars on I-30 bounced off the grooved metal siding of the structure, and it was hot to the touch.

"Is this it?" the fat man uttered softly.

"Quiet!"

Travis felt that the fat man should know what was happening according to his reactions. He stuck his head around the corner. There was a concrete slab at the foot of the entrance to the building, but more importantly, no tin cover.

"Come on."

Travis was much hastier in getting to the door of the second warehouse. He was getting so close to Mike now, his stealth was suffering. A full trot now. The fat man was having trouble keeping up. He tripped over a jointed outside pipe that had been covered by the overgrowth.

"Oh, c'mon! Get up, man!" Travis whispered as loudly as he could.

"Don't worry about me, keep going," he was a little embarrassed.

Travis knew that this was the building. As he came upon the corner and looked around, he saw the metal easement over a single glass door. Parked out front was an early eighties model grey sedan. The paint was peeling and the tires were bald. Travis moved to the door and tried to take a quick glance inside. It was too dark inside and the door was too dirty to make anything out. He pulled on the handle. It was open. The fat man stepped in front of Travis.

"Take a step back."

Travis was relieved that the keystone cop appeared to have put aside his bumbling diffidence. He let him take the lead as they entered the warehouse. There was a stark contrast between the dark, shadowy areas of the warehouse and the patches that were illuminated by the invasive beams of sunlight. The sawdust and other airborne elements in the light further impeded their view. The visibility was no more than twenty-five yards. They moved forward at a snail's pace. The air was stale and humid. The fat man had shed his suit jacket and his shirt was soaked in sweat. Travis felt the beads rolling down his face as well.

"Whoever is holding my daughter and the young man, come on out and we can talk about this. There's no need for anybody to get hurt."

The fat man's voice caromed off the walls of the indoor canyon.

"Daddy?"

The daughter responded to her father's voice.

"Honey! Where are you, sweetheart?"

Travis knew the fat man had taken the wrong approach. Any man who would associate with Figg wasn't going to be amenable to negotiating. And like a scared badger backed into a corner, the driver was likely going to come out lunging, claws first.

The next sound was a gunshot. The fat man's body did a one hundred and eighty degree spin. Before he fell to the ground, Travis made out a wound exposing the fat man's pectoral muscle tissue and part of a rib. Travis hit the deck. He held his rifle above his head and went into a series of rolls until his body was stopped by a two foot high tarp-covered obstruction. He scrambled over it and gained cover. The fat man's daughter was crying uncontrollably from the sound of the gunshot. Travis kept quiet. He wasn't sure if the driver had seen him or not. Travis held loosely to the hope that the driver might not think he was with the fat man, or that he hadn't seen him.

"If you're there, kid, I suggest you go ahead and drop your weapon and come out into the open," he quickly debunked Travis' hypothetical and moved the first pawn.

Travis wasn't going to move just yet. He remained silent.

"Your brother would really appreciate your cooperation, trust me on that."

The driver moved a second piece. His voice was husky and heavy on bass.

"Travis…Travis are you out there?"

Travis' heart skipped three beats hearing Mike's voice. He felt a combination of joy, relief and fear. It made it almost impossible to keep up his bluff. He felt the words going from his brain to his tongue like a race car on the German autobahn. Somehow, he managed to slam on the brakes. He kept quiet. There was nary a word spoken for the next few minutes. The fat man's daughter was still crying. Travis turned onto his back, fished through his pocket and pulled out the second and final bullet. He softly bolted it through so as to not give away his position. He rested the barrel of the AR-15 atop the tarp. The scope gave him an immeasurable visual advantage. He slowly panned left and then back to the right. Within a few seconds, he made out overlapping figures coming through the saw-dusty haze. It was Mike and the driver. Using Mike's body as a shield, he held a gun to his head and came to a stop. He was enormous, even bigger than Mike. He bulged out on either side of him.

"Do you want to watch me blow this retard's head off, kid?"

Apparently, the driver wasn't going to take a chance biting on a bluff, and went ahead and checked with his king-piece. They were standing roughly fifty yards away. A large, forty-five degree beam of sunlight bisected their bodies, diagonally, at the waist. Travis molested them both with the scope's crosshair.

"C'mon, give me just a *little* bit," he thought to himself.

His adrenaline was pumping so violently, he never stopped to realize that he had conquered the demons that had haunted him since he first held a scope to his eye.

"I'll spread his brain all over this floor."

The driver's voice was laced with desperation. He had been reduced to bargaining his way out of the warehouse with his head still connected to his shoulders. Travis continued probing for a clean shot. Whispering to himself helped to calm his nerves.

"C'mon you bastard, turn this way just a little."

Another twenty seconds passed. Then, the driver made the last decision of his life. It was a stunningly poor one. Travis was shocked, and pleased, at the enormity of the shot the target had given him. The entire side of his head landed on the crosshairs nexus. There was a high velocity, red splash as both bodies fell from view. It was checkmate. Travis crawled over the tarp.

"Mikey!"

"Mikey!"

"Travis?"

Mike crawled out from underneath the driver's headless corpse. The entire left side of his face and body were covered in blood. Travis saw him and broke down. He tossed the rifle aside and leapt over the tarp cover. His eyes filled with tears as he sprinted to and embraced his big brother. Mike returned the hug and lifted him six inches off the ground.

"Mike, I told you I'd be back."

"Hey Trav, where have you been? Are you still a part of the show?"

Travis laughed as he wiped away tears.

"Yeah, buddy, I'm still part of the show. But it's over now. We can go home."

He hugged his big brother more tightly than he ever had before.

Another shot rang out.

Travis felt a sharp pain in his gut. He slid down Mike's body and landed on his knees. He looked at his mid-section. Blood spread all over the cotton cloth of his T-shirt. He looked up at Mike. His face was blank. He looked at Mike's right hand. He had taken the driver's gun. Mike fell to his knees to be eye-to-eye with his brother.

"Hey Trav, I'm the hero! I'm the hero!"

Travis coughed up blood.

"*What*? ...what've you done, Mike?" He gargled the ruby syrup.

"They told me that if I shot you, I'd be the hero of the show. It's just like 'bank robbery', Trav, remember when we were little? I bet you didn't think I remembered that game, did you?"

Figg had made one, final move in their game of chess from beyond the grave. Travis couldn't hide the sadness from his face as he saw the innocence in his brother's eyes. He fell onto his side and rolled onto his back. He coughed up more blood. Mike shuffled over on his knees to Travis' side.

"Why is there blood coming out of your mouth, Trav?"

"Mikey, Mikey. They were right. You *are* the hero. You'll always be the hero. You think you can remember that? You'll *always* be the hero."

"Yeah, I'll remember. Can we go home now? Get up and we'll go home. I think the show is over and I'm really tired of this place. Besides, I really want a double scoop of chocolate ice cream right now. C'mon, let's go."

"I'll tell you what," Travis winced as the bile rushed to the bullet-pierced cavity in his stomach. "Go get that little girl and make sure she's okay. Can you do that for me?"

"Yeah, but you know I don't like girls, Trav."

"Yeah, I know, but she needs you're help. I want you to take her to Cubby and I'll catch up with you, okay? Keep walking until you get there. Don't stop no matter what and don't wait up for me. I'll be there soon enough. I just need to rest for a few minutes."

"Okay, but don't be too long. We need to get home."

Travis struggled to raise his head. He spotted the fat man's body some thirty feet away.

"Listen to me, Mike. Are you listening?"

"Yeah."

"Mikey, look me in the eyes," Travis wanted to be sure he had Mike's undivided attention. "When you take the little girl outta' here, I want you to walk along the wall over here, behind me," he pointed to the wall where they could leave the warehouse without the girl having to see her father, who had ceased to be.

"I want you to let her stand right next to the wall and you stand on the other side of her. Do you understand me, Mikey? It's very important."

"Yeah, I guess so."

"Keep walking until you get there. Don't stop no matter what and don't wait up for me. I'll be there soon enough."

Mike retrieved the fat man's daughter and headed towards the door. Travis was filled with a slew of final thoughts as the clouds started to cover his peripheral vision.

"Dad, can you hear me? I guess I disappointed you some. I tried to live by the code, but I fell short at times. I think about you a lot. More than you know. I did my best to take care of Mikey, he seems to be doin' okay, everything considered. I'm turning him over to someone I know you would've liked. He'll take good care of him. Maybe I'll be seeing you here pretty soon. I'd really like that. I've missed you."

His thoughts turned to Cub.

"Well, Cub, it looks like maybe Hobbes was closer to the truth than you thought. He probably didn't have the inherent evil of someone like Figg in mind when he described man, though. I'll miss you, old friend. I'm scared, Cub. Not of dying, but of leaving Mike behind. I hope you'll look after him. Ya' know, make sure he stays outta' trouble and stuff. It's not as easy as you might think. I mean, look at me. I made my share of mistakes, but in the end, I kept him alive and relatively unafraid. But above all, you've got to be..."

Before Mike and the little girl were halfway to the door, Travis exhaled for the final time.

"I'll see ya' back at Cub's, Trav," Mike cried out.

"Don't rest for too long, okay?-Okay!"

He continued to bark instructions to his dead brother as he took the little girl by the hand and left the building.

The silence of death filled the industrial mausoleum as Travis, the fat man and the driver's bodies all leaked blood. In the middle of the massive concrete slab laid the snitch, lifeless, on the filth-laden floor of a barren, superfluous warehouse in southeast Dallas. His eyes wide with the empty, glazed over quality that is the final curtain. Despite the worry that had consumed his last seconds, there appeared to be a tranquility flowing over his face. Maybe it was contentment. When all was said and done, he had accomplished *his* objective. Outside, Mike and the little girl slowly began to walk back in the direction of the Beast. She had finally stopped crying.

"Where's my dad?" She asked.

Mike didn't understand why she would ask such a question. Instead of answering, he went to his small stable of opening lines when conversing with a stranger.

"Do you like ice cream?"

"Yes," she answered, sniffling, fragile.

"Me too. Especially chocolate, double scoop. What's your name?"

"Samantha."

"My name is Mikey. I'm the hero of the show. That's my brother back there in that place. He's gonna' meet up with us later."

"Where are we going?" she asked.

"We're goin' to see Cubby. My brother told me we were supposed to go see Cubby. Do you know Cubby?"

"No."

"He's me and Travis' friend,"

"Can he call my mommy?" she asked.

"I guess. I know where there's a phone you can use that's close to my home."

They walked hand in hand, the giant, vulnerable vagabond and his intellectual peer. Above them, the traffic whizzed along on the Interstate.

Printed in the United States
1418200002B/62

9 781592 680450